By C. S. Lewis:

*The Abolition of Man*

*Mere Christianity*

*The Great Divorce*

*The Problem of Pain*

*The Weight of Glory and Other Addresses*

*The Screwtape Letters* (with "Screwtape Proposes a Toast")

*Miracles*

*The Case for Christianity*

*The Lion, the Witch and the Wardrobe*

*Prince Caspian*

*The Voyage of the Dawn Treader*

*The Silver Chair*

*The Magician's Nephew*

*The Horse and His Boy*

*The Last Battle*

*Perelandra*

*That Hideous Strength*

*Out of the Silent Planet*

*The Joyful Christian*

*George Macdonald: An Anthology*


About C. S. Lewis:

*Through Joy and Beyond: A Pictorial Biography of C. S. Lewis*, by Walter Hooper

*Past Watchful Dragons: The Narnian Chronicles of C. S. Lewis*, by Walter Hooper

*They Stand Together: The Letters of C. S. Lewis to Arthur Greeves (1914-1963)*, edited by Walter Hooper

*C. S. Lewis at the Breakfast Table and Other Reminiscences*, edited by James T. Como

Available at your local bookstore or from Macmillan Publishing Co., Inc., 100K Brown Street, Riverside, NJ 08370

C. S. LEWIS

# Out of the Silent Planet

*Macmillan Publishing Co., Inc.*

NEW YORK

Macmillan Paperbacks Edition 1965

35   34   33

ISBN 0-02-086880-4

Macmillan Publishing Co., Inc.
866 Third Avenue, New York, N.Y. 10022

*To*

MY BROTHER W. H. L.

*a life-long critic of the space-and-time story*

NOTE: *Certain slighting references to earlier stories of this type which will be found in the following pages have been put there for purely dramatic purposes. The author would be sorry if any reader supposed he was too stupid to have enjoyed Mr. H. G. Wells's fantasies or too ungrateful to acknowledge his debt to them.*

C. S. L.

# Chapter 1

THE LAST DROPS of the thundershower had hardly ceased falling when the Pedestrian stuffed his map into his pocket, settled his pack more comfortably on his tired shoulders, and stepped out from the shelter of a large chestnut-tree into the middle of the road. A violent yellow sunset was pouring through a rift in the clouds to westward, but straight ahead over the hills the sky was the colour of dark slate. Every tree and blade of grass was dripping, and the road shone like a river. The Pedestrian wasted no time on the landscape but set out at once with the determined stride of a good walker who has lately realized that he will have to walk farther than he intended. That, indeed, was his situation. If he had chosen to look back, which he did not, he could have seen the spire of Much Nadderby, and, seeing it, might have uttered a malediction on the inhospitable little hotel which, though obviously empty, had refused him a bed. The place had changed hands since he last went for a walking-tour in these parts. The kindly old landlord on whom he had reckoned had been replaced by someone whom the barmaid referred to as 'the lady,' and the lady was apparently a British innkeeper of that orthodox school who regard guests as a nuisance. His only chance now was Sterk, on the far side of the hills, and a good six miles away. The map marked an inn at Sterk. The Pedestrian was too experienced to build any very sanguine hopes on this, but there seemed nothing else within range.

He walked fairly fast, and doggedly, without looking much about him, like a man trying to shorten the way with some interesting train of thought. He was tall, but a little round-shouldered, about thirty-five to forty years of age, and dressed with that particular kind of shabbiness which marks a member of the intelligentsia on a holiday. He might easily have been mistaken for a doctor or a schoolmaster at first sight, though he had not the man-of-the-world air of the one or the indefinable breeziness of the other. In fact, he was a philologist, and fellow of a Cambridge college. His name was Ransom.

He had hoped when he left Nadderby that he might find a night's lodging at some friendly farm before he had walked as far as Sterk. But the land this side of the hills seemed almost uninhabited. It was a desolate, featureless sort of country mainly devoted to cabbage and turnip, with poor hedges and few trees. It attracted no visitors like the richer country south of Nadderby and it was protected by the hills from the industrial areas beyond Sterk. As the evening drew in and the noise of the birds came to an end it grew more silent than an English landscape usually is. The noise of his own feet on the metalled road became irritating.

He had walked thus for a matter of two miles when he became aware of a light ahead. He was close under the hills by now and it was nearly dark, so that he still cherished hopes of a substantial farmhouse until he was quite close to the real origin of the light, which proved to be a very small cottage of ugly nineteenth-century brick. A woman darted out of the open doorway as he approached it and almost collided with him.

'I beg your pardon, sir,' she said. 'I thought it was my Harry.'

Ransom asked her if there was any place nearer than Sterk where he might possibly get a bed.

'No, sir,' said the woman. 'Not nearer than Sterk. I dare say as they might fix you up at Nadderby.'

She spoke in a humbly fretful voice as if her mind were intent on something else. Ransom explained that he had already tried Nadderby.

'Then I don't know, I'm sure, sir,' she replied. 'There isn't hardly any house before Sterk, not what you want. There's only The Rise, where my Harry works, and I thought you was coming from that way, sir, and that's why I come out when I heard you, thinking it might be him. He ought to be home this long time.'

'The Rise,' said Ransom. 'What's that? A farm? Would they put me up?'

'Oh no, sir. You see there's no one there now except the Professor and the gentleman from London, not since Miss Alice died. They wouldn't do anything like that, sir. They don't even keep any servants, except my Harry for doing the furnace like, and he's not in the house.'

'What's this professor's name?' asked Ransom, with a faint hope.

'I don't know, I'm sure, sir,' said the woman. 'The other gentleman's Mr. Devine, he is, and Harry says the *other* gentleman is a professor. He don't know much about it, you see, sir, being a little simple, and that's why I don't like him coming home so late, and they said they'd always send him home at six o'clock. It isn't as if he didn't do a good day's work either.'

The monotonous voice and the limited range of the woman's vocabulary did not express much emotion, but Ransom was standing sufficiently near to perceive that she was trembling and nearly crying. It occurred to him that he ought to call on the mysterious professor and ask for the boy to be sent home: and it occurred to him just a fraction of a second later that once he were inside the house—among men of his own profession—he might very reasonably accept the offer of a night's hospitality. Whatever the process of thought may have been, he found that the mental picture of himself calling at The Rise had assumed all the solidity of a thing determined upon. He told the woman what he intended to do.

'Thank you very much, sir, I'm sure,' she said. 'And if you would be so kind as to see him out of the gate and on the road before you leave, if you see what I mean, sir. He's that frightened of the Professor and he wouldn't come away once your back was turned, sir, not if they hadn't sent him home themselves like.'

Ransom reassured the woman as well as he could and bade her good-bye, after ascertaining that he would find The Rise on his left in about five minutes. Stiffness had grown upon him while he was standing still, and he proceeded slowly and painfully on his way.

There was no sign of any lights on the left of the road—nothing but the flat fields and a mass of darkness which he took to be a copse. It seemed more than five minutes before he reached it and found that he had been mistaken. It was divided from the road by a good hedge and in the hedge was a white gate: and the trees which rose above him as he examined the gate were not the first line of a copse but only a belt, and the sky showed through them. He felt quite sure now that this must be the gate of The Rise and that these trees surrounded a house and garden. He tried the gate and found it locked. He stood for a moment undecided, discouraged by the silence and the growing darkness. His first inclination, tired as he felt, was to continue his journey to Sterk: but he had committed himself to a troublesome duty on behalf of the old woman. He knew that it would be possible, if one really wanted, to force a way through the hedge. He did not want to. A nice fool he would look, blundering in upon some retired eccentric—the sort of a man who kept his gates locked in the country—with this silly story of a hysterical mother in tears because her idiot boy had been kept half an hour late at his work! Yet it was perfectly clear that he would have to get in, and since one cannot crawl through a hedge with a pack on, he slipped his pack off and flung it over the gate. The moment he had done so, it seemed to him that he had not till now fully made up his mind —now that he must break into the garden if only in order to recover the pack. He became very angry with the woman, and with himself, but he got down on his hands and knees and began to worm his way into the hedge.

The operation proved more difficult that he had expected and it was several minutes before he stood up in the wet darkness on the inner side of the hedge smarting from his contact with thorns and nettles. He groped his way to the gate, picked up his pack, and then for the first time turned to take stock of his surroundings. It was lighter on the drive than it had been under the trees and he had no difficulty in making out a large stone house divided from him by a width of untidy neglected lawn. The drive branched into two a little way ahead of him— the righthand path leading in a gentle sweep to the front door, while the left ran straight ahead, doubtless to the back premises of the house. He noticed that this path was churned up into deep ruts—now full of water—as if it were used to carrying a traffic of heavy lorries. The other, on which he now began to approach the house, was overgrown with moss. The house itself showed no light: some of the windows were shuttered, some gaped blank without shutter or curtain, but all were lifeless and inhospitable. The only sign of occupation was a column of smoke that rose from behind the house with a density which suggested the chimney of a factory, or at least of a laundry, rather than that of a kitchen. The Rise was clearly the last place in the world where a stranger was likely to be asked to stay the night, and Ransom, who had already wasted some time in exploring it, would certainly have turned away if he had not been bound by his unfortunate promise to the old woman.

He mounted the three steps which led into the deep porch, rang the bell, and waited. After a time he rang the bell again and sat down on a wooden bench which ran along one side of the porch. He sat so long that though the night was warm and starlit the sweat began to dry on his face and a faint chilliness crept over his shoulders. He was very tired by now, and it was perhaps this which prevented him from rising and ringing a third time: this, and the soothing stillness of the garden, the beauty of the summer sky, and the occasional hooting of an owl somewhere in the neighbourhood which seemed only to emphasize the underlying tranquillity of his surroundings. Something like drowsiness had already descended upon him when he found himself startled into vigilance. A peculiar noise was going on—a scuffing, irregular noise, vaguely reminiscent of a football scrum. He stood up. The noise was unmistakable by now. People in boots were fighting or wrestling or playing some game. They were shouting too. He could not make out the words but he heard the monosyllabic barking ejaculations of men who are angry and out of breath. The last thing Ransom wanted was an adventure, but a conviction that he ought to investigate the matter was already growing upon him when a much louder cry rang out in which he could distinguish the words, 'Let me go. Let me go,' and then, a second later, 'I'm not going in there. Let me go home.'

Throwing off his pack, Ransom sprang down the steps of the porch, and ran round to the back of the house as quickly as his stiff and footsore condition allowed him. The ruts and pools of the muddy path led him to what seemed to be a yard, but a yard surrounded with an unusual number of outhouses. He had a momentary vision of a tall chimney, a low door filled with red firelight, and a huge round shape that rose black against the stars, which he took for the dome of a small observatory: then all this was blotted out of his mind by the figures of three men who were struggling together so close to him that he almost cannoned into them. From the very first Ransom felt no doubt that the central figure, whom the two others seemed to be detaining in spite of his struggles, was the old woman's Harry. He would like to have thundered out, 'What are you doing to that boy?' but the words that actually came— in rather an unimpressive voice—were, 'Here! I say! . . .'

The three combatants fell suddenly apart, the boy blubbering. 'May I ask,' said the thicker and taller of the two men, 'who the devil you may be and what you are doing here?' His voice had all the qualities which Ransom's had so regrettably lacked.

'I'm on a walking-tour,' said Ransom, 'and I promised a poor woman——'

'Poor woman be damned,' said the other. 'How did you get in?'

'Through the hedge,' said Ransom, who felt a little ill-temper coming to his assistance. 'I don't know what you're doing to that boy, but——'

'We ought to have a dog in this place,' said the thick man to his companion, ignoring Ransom.

'You mean we should have a dog if you hadn't insisted on using Tartar for an experiment,' said the man who had not yet spoken. He was nearly as tall as the other, but slender, and apparently the younger of the two, and his voice sounded vaguely familiar to Ransom.

The latter made a fresh beginning. 'Look here,' he said. 'I don't know what you are doing to that boy, but it's long after hours and it is high time you sent him home. I haven't the least wish to interfere in your private affairs, but——'

'Who are you?' bawled the thick man.

'My name is Ransom, if that is what you mean. And——'

'By Jove,' said the slender man, 'not Ransom who used to be at Wedenshaw?'

' I was at school at Wedenshaw,' said Ransom.

'I thought I knew you as soon as you spoke,' said the slender man. 'I'm Devine. Don't you remember me?'

'Of course. I should think I do!' said Ransom as the two

men shook hands with the rather laboured cordiality which is traditional in such meetings. In actual fact Ransom had disliked Devine at school as much as anyone he could remember.

'Touching, isn't it?' said Devine. 'The far-flung line even in the wilds of Sterk and Nadderby. This is where we get a lump in our throats and remember Sunday-evening Chapel in the D.O.P. You don't know Weston, perhaps?' Devine indicated his massive and loud-voiced companion. '*The* Weston,' he added. 'You know. The great physicist. Has Einstein on toast and drinks a pint of Schrödinger's blood for breakfast. Weston, allow me to introduce my old schoolfellow, Ransom. Dr. Elwin Ransom. *The* Ransom, you know. The great philologist. Has Jespersen on toast and drinks a pint——'

'I know nothing about it,' said Weston, who was still holding the unfortunate Harry by the collar. 'And if you expect me to say that I am pleased to see this person who has just broken into my garden, you will be disappointed. I don't care twopence what school he was at nor on what unscientific foolery he is at present wasting money that ought to go to research. I want to know what he's doing here: and after that I want to see the last of him.'

'Don't be an ass, Weston,' said Devine in a more serious voice. 'His dropping in is delightfully apropos. You mustn't mind Weston's little way, Ransom. Conceals a generous heart beneath a grim exterior, you know. You'll come in and have a drink and something to eat of course?'

'That's very kind of you,' said Ransom. 'But about the boy——'

Devine drew Ransom aside. 'Balmy,' he said in a low voice. 'Works like a beaver as a rule but gets these fits. We are only trying to get him into the wash-house and keep him quiet for an hour or so till he's normal again. Can't let him go home in his present state. All done by kindness. You can take him home yourself presently if you like—and come back and sleep here.'

Ransom was very much perplexed. There was something about the whole scene suspicious enough and disagreeable enough to convince him the he had blundered on something criminal, while on the other hand he had all the deep, irrational conviction of his age and class that such things could never cross the path of an ordinary person except in fiction and could least of all be associated with professors and old schoolfellows. Even if they had been ill-treating the boy, Ransom did not see much chance of getting him from them by force.

While these thoughts were passing through his head, Devine had been speaking to Weston, in a low voice, but no lower than was to be expected of a man discussing hospitable arrangements in the presence of a guest. It ended with a grunt of assent from Weston. Ransom, to whose other difficulties a merely social embarrassment was now being added, turned with the idea of making some remark. But Weston was now speaking to the boy.

'You have given enough trouble for one night, Harry,' he said. 'And in a properly governed country I'd know how to deal with you. Hold your tongue and stop snivelling. You needn't go into the wash-house if you don't want——'

'It weren't the wash-house,' sobbed the half-wit, 'you know it weren't. I don't want to go in *that* thing again.'

'He means the laboratory,' interrupted Devine. 'He got in there and was shut in by accident for a few hours once. It put the wind up him for some reason. Lo, the poor Indian, you know.' He turned to the boy. 'Listen, Harry,' he said. 'That kind gentleman is going to take you home as soon as he's had a rest. If you'll come in and sit down quietly in the hall I'll give you something you like.' He imitated the noise of a cork being drawn from a bottle—Ransom remembered it had been one of Devine's tricks at school—and a guffaw of infantile knowingness broke from Harry's lips.

'Bring him in,' said Weston as he turned away and disappeared into the house. Ransom hesitated to follow, but Devine assured him that Weston would be very glad to see him. The lie was barefaced, but Ransom's desire for a rest and a drink were rapidly overcoming his social scruples. Preceded by Devine and Harry, he entered the house and found himself a moment later seated in an arm-chair and awaiting the return of Devine, who had gone to fetch refreshments.

# Chapter 2

THE ROOM into which he had been shown revealed a strange mixture of luxury and squalor. The windows were shuttered and curtainless, the floor was uncarpeted and strewn with packing-cases, shavings, newspapers and boots, and the wall-paper showed the stains left by the pictures and furniture of the previous occupants. On the other hand, the only two arm-chairs were of the costliest type, and in the litter which covered the tables, cigars, oyster-shells and empty champagne-bottles jostled with tins of condensed milk and opened sardine-tins, with cheap crockery, broken bread, and teacups a quarter full of tea and cigarette-ends.

His hosts seemed to be a long time away, and Ransom fell to thinking of Devine. He felt for him that sort of distaste we feel for someone whom we have admired in boyhood for a very brief period and then outgrown. Devine had learned just half a term earlier than anyone else that kind of humour which consists in a perpetual parody of the sentimental or idealistic clichés of one's elders. For a few weeks his references to the Dear Old Place and to Playing the Game, to the White Man's Burden and a Straight Bat, had swept everyone, Ransom included, off their feet. But before he left Wedenshaw Ransom had already begun to find Devine a bore, and at Cambridge he had avoided him, wondering from afar how anyone so flashy and, as it were, ready-made, could be so successful. Then had come the mystery of Devine's election to the Leicester fellowship, and the further mystery of his increasing wealth. He had long since abandoned Cambridge for London, and was presumably something 'in the city.' One heard of him occasionally and one's informant usually ended either by saying, 'A damn clever chap, Devine, in his own way,' or else by observing plaintively, 'It's a mystery to me how that man has got where he is.' As far as Ransom could gather from their brief conversation in the yard, his old schoolfellow had altered very little.

He was interrupted by the opening of the door. Devine

entered alone, carrying a bottle of whiskey on a tray with glasses, and a syphon.

'Weston is looking out something to eat,' he said as he placed the tray on the floor beside Ransom's chair, and addressed himself to opening the bottle. Ransom, who was very thirsty indeed by now, observed that his host was one of those irritating people who forget to use their hands when they begin talking. Devine started to prise up the silver paper which covered the cork with the point of a corkscrew, and then stopped to ask:

'How do you come to be in this benighted part of the country?'

'I'm on a walking-tour,' said Ransom; 'slept at Stoke Underwood last night and had hoped to end at Nadderby to-night. They wouldn't put me up, so I was going on to Sterk.'

'God!' exclaimed Devine, his corkscrew still idle. 'Do you do it for money, or is it sheer masochism?'

'Pleasure, of course,' said Ransom, keeping his eye immovably on the still unopened bottle.

'Can the attraction of it be explained to the uninitiate?' asked Devine, remembering himself sufficiently to rip up a small portion of the silver paper.

'I hardly know. To begin with, I like the actual walking——'

'God! You must have enjoyed the army. Jogging along to Thingummy, eh?'

'No, no. It's just the opposite of the army. The whole point about the army is that you are never alone for a moment and can never choose where you're going or even what part of the road you're walking on. On a walking-tour you are absolutely detached. You stop where you like and go on when you like. As long as it lasts you need consider no one and consult no one but yourself.'

'Until one night you find a wire waiting at your hotel saying, "Come back at once," ' replied Devine, at last removing the silver paper.

'Only if you were fool enough to leave a list of addresses and go to them! The worst that could happen to me would be that man on the wireless saying, "Will Dr. Elwin Ransom, believed to be walking somewhere in the Midlands——" '

'I begin to see the idea,' said Devine, pausing in the very

act of drawing the cork. 'It wouldn't do if you were in business. You are a lucky devil! But can even you just disappear
like that? No wife, no young, no aged but honest parent or
anything of that sort?'

'Only a married sister in India. And then, you see, I'm a
don. And a don in the middle of long vacation is almost a
non-existent creature, as you ought to remember. College
neither knows nor cares where he is, and certainly no one
else does.'

The cork at last came out of the bottle with a heart-cheering
noise.

'Say when,' said Devine, as Ransom held out his glass. 'But
I feel sure there's a catch somewhere. Do you really mean
to say that no one knows where you are or when you ought
to get back, and no one can get hold of you?'

Ransom was nodding in reply when Devine, who had
picked up the syphon, suddenly swore. 'I'm afraid this is
empty,' he said. 'Do you mind having water? I'll have to get
some from the scullery. How much do you like?'

'Fill it up please,' said Ransom.

A few minutes later Devine returned and handed Ransom
his long-delayed drink. The latter remarked, as he put down
the half-emptied tumbler with a sigh of satisfaction, that
Devine's choice of residence was at least as odd as his own
choice of a holiday.

'Quite,' said Devine. 'But if you knew Weston you'd realize
that it's much less trouble to go where he wants than to argue
the matter. What you call a strong colleague.'

'Colleague?' said Ransom inquiringly.

'In a sense.' Devine glanced at the door, drew his chair
closer to Ransom's, and continued in a more confidential
tone. 'He's the goods all right, though. Between ourselves, I
am putting a little money into some experiments he has on
hand. It's all straight stuff—the march of progress and the
good of humanity and all that, but it has an industrial side.'

While Devine was speaking something odd began to happen
to Ransom. At first it merely seemed to him that Devine's
words were no longer making sense. He appeared to be saying
that he was industrial all down both sides but could never
get an experiment to fit him in London. Then he realized

that Devine was not so much unintelligible as inaudible, which was not surprising, since he was now so far away—about a mile away, though perfectly clear like something seen through the wrong end of a telescope. From that bright distance where he sat in his tiny chair he was gazing at Ransom with a new expression on his face. The gaze became disconcerting. Ransom tried to move in his chair but found that he had lost all power over his own body. He felt quite comfortable, but it was as if his legs and arms had been bandaged to the chair and his head gripped in a vice; a beautifully padded, but quite immovable vice. He did not feel afraid, though he knew that he ought to be afraid and soon would be. Then, very gradually, the room faded from his sight.

Ransom could never be sure whether what followed had any bearing on the events recorded in this book or whether it was merely an irresponsible dream. It seemed to him that he and Weston and Devine were all standing in a little garden surrounded by a wall. The garden was bright and sunlit, but over the top of the wall you could see nothing but darkness. They were trying to climb over the wall and Weston asked them to give him a hoist up. Ransom kept on telling him not to go over the wall because it was so dark on the other side, but Weston insisted, and all three of them set about doing so. Ransom was the last. He got astride on the top of the wall, sitting on his coat because of the broken bottles. The other two had already dropped down on the outside into the darkness, but before he followed them a door in the wall—which none of them had noticed—was opened from without and the queerest people he had ever seen came into the garden bringing Weston and Devine back with them. They left them in the garden and retired into the darkness themselves, locking the door behind them. Ransom found it impossible to get down from the wall. He remained sitting there, not frightened but rather uncomfortable because his right leg, which was on the outside, felt so dark and his left leg felt so light. 'My leg will drop off if it gets much darker,' he said. Then he looked down into the darkness and asked, 'Who are you?' and the Queer People must still have been there for they all replied, 'Hoo—Hoo—Hoo?' just like owls.

He began to realize that his leg was not so much dark as

cold and stiff, because he had been resting the other on it for so long: and also that he was in an arm-chair in a lighted room. A conversation was going on near him and had, he now realized, been going on for some time. His head was comparatively clear. He realized that he had been drugged or hypnotized, or both, and he felt that some control over his own body was returning to him though he was still very weak. He listened intently without trying to move.

'I'm getting a little tired of this, Weston,' Devine was saying, 'and specially as it's my money that is being risked. I tell you he'll do quite as well as the boy, and in some ways better. Only, he'll be coming round very soon now and we must get him on board at once. We ought to have done it an hour ago.'

'The boy was ideal,' said Weston sulkily. 'Incapable of serving humanity and only too likely to propagate idiocy. He was the sort of boy who in a civilized community would be automatically handed over to a state laboratory for experimental purposes.'

'I dare say. But in England he is the sort of boy in whom Scotland Yard might conceivably feel an interest. This busybody, on the other hand, will not be missed for months, and even then no one will know where he was when he disappeared. He came alone. He left no address. He has no family. And finally he has poked his nose into the whole affair of his own accord.'

'Well, I confess I don't like it. He is, after all, human. The boy was really almost a—a preparation. Still, he's only an individual, and probably a quite useless one. We're risking our own lives too. In a great cause——'

'For the Lord's sake don't start all that stuff now. We haven't time.'

'I dare say,' replied Weston, 'he would consent if he could be made to understand.'

'Take his feet and I'll take his head,' said Devine.

'If you really think he's coming round,' said Weston, 'you'd better give him another dose. We can't start till we get the sunlight. It wouldn't be pleasant to have him struggling in there for three hours or so. It would be better if he didn't wake up till we were under weigh.'

'True enough. Just keep an eye on him while I run upstairs and get another.'

Devine left the room. Ransom saw through his half-closed eyes that Weston was standing over him. He had no means of foretelling how his own body would respond, if it responded at all, to a sudden attempt of movement, but he saw at once that he must take his chance. Almost before Devine had closed the door he flung himself with all his force at Weston's feet. The scientist fell forward across the chair, and Ransom, flinging him off with an agonizing effort, rose and dashed out into the hall. He was very weak and fell as he entered it: but terror was behind him and in a couple of seconds he had found the hall door and was working desperately to master the bolts. Darkness and his trembling hands were against him. Before he had drawn one bolt, booted feet were clattering over the carpetless floor behind him. He was gripped by the shoulders and the knees. Kicking, writhing, dripping with sweat, and bellowing as loud as he could in the faint hope of rescue, he prolonged the struggle with a violence of which he would have believed himself incapable. For one glorious moment the door was open, the fresh night air was in his face, he saw the reassuring stars and even his own pack lying in the porch. Then a heavy blow fell on his head. Consciousness faded, and the last thing of which he was aware was the grip of strong hands pulling him back into the dark passage, and the sound of a closing door.

## Chapter 3

WHEN RANSOM came to his senses he seemed to be in bed in a dark room. He had a pretty severe headache, and this, combined with a general lassitude, discouraged him at first from attempting to rise or to take stock of his surroundings. He noticed, drawing his hand across his forehead, that he was sweating freely, and this directed his attention to the fact that the room (if it was a room) was remarkably warm. Moving his arms to fling off the bedclothes, he touched a wall at the right side of the bed: it was not only warm, but hot. He moved his left hand to and fro in the emptiness on the other side and noticed that there the air was cooler—apparently the heat was coming from the wall. He felt his face and found a bruise over the left eye. This recalled to his mind the struggle with Weston and Devine, and he instantly concluded that they had put him in an outhouse behind their furnace. At the same time he looked up and recognized the source of the dim light in which, without noticing it, he had all along been able to see the movements of his own hands. There was some kind of skylight immediately over his head—a square of night sky filled with stars. It seemed to Ransom that he had never looked out on such a frosty night. Pulsing with brightness as with some unbearable pain or pleasure, clustered in pathless and countless multitudes, dreamlike in clarity, blazing in perfect blackness, the stars seized all his attention, troubled him, excited him, and drew him up to a sitting position. At the same time they quickened the throb of his headache, and this reminded him that he had been drugged. He was just formulating to himself the theory that the stuff they had given him might have some effect on the pupil and that this would explain the unnatural splendour and fullness of the sky, when a disturbance of silver light, almost a pale and miniature sunrise, at one corner of the skylight, drew his eyes upward again. Some minutes later the orb of the full moon was pushing its way into the field of vision. Ransom sat still and watched. He had never seen such a moon—so

21

white, so blinding and so large. 'Like a great football just outside the glass,' he thought, and then, a moment later, 'No —it's bigger than that.' By this time he was quite certain that something was seriously wrong with his eyes: no moon could possibly be the size of the thing he was seeing.

The light of the huge moon—if it was a moon—had by now illuminated his surroundings almost as clearly as if it were day. It was a very strange room. The floor was so small that the bed and a table beside it occupied the whole width of it: the ceiling seemed to be nearly twice as wide and the walls sloped outwards as they rose, so that Ransom had the impression of lying at the bottom of a deep and narrow wheelbarrow. This confirmed his belief that his sight was either temporarily or permanently injured. In other respects, however, he was recovering rapidly and even beginning to feel an unnatural lightness of heart and a not disagreeable excitement. The heat was still oppressive, and he stripped off everything but his shirt and trousers before rising to explore. His rising was disastrous and raised graver apprehensions in his mind about the effects of being drugged. Although he had been conscious of no unusual muscular effort, he found himself leaping from the bed with an energy which brought his head into sharp contact with the skylight and flung him down again in a heap on the floor. He found himself on the other side against the wall—the wall that ought to have sloped outwards like the side of a wheelbarrow, according to his previous reconnaissance. But it didn't. He felt it and looked at it: it was unmistakably at right angles to the floor. More cautiously this time, he rose again to his feet. He felt an extraordinary lightness of body: it was with difficulty that he kept his feet on the floor. For the first time a suspicion that he might be dead and already in the ghost-life crossed his mind. He was trembling, but a hundred mental habits forbade him to consider this possibility. Instead, he explored his prison. The result was beyond doubt: all the walls looked as if they sloped outwards so as to make the room wider at the ceiling than it was at the floor, but each wall as you stood beside it turned out to be perfectly perpendicular—not only to sight but to touch also if one stooped down and examined with one's fingers the angle between it and the floor. The same examination revealed two other curious facts. The room was walled and floored with metal, and was in a state of continuous faint vibration—a silent vibration with a strangely life-like and unmechanical quality about it. But if the vibration was silent, there was plenty of noise going on—a series of musical raps or percussions at quite irregular intervals which seemed to come from the ceiling. It was as if the metal chamber in which he found himself was being bombarded with small, tinkling missiles. Ransom was by now thoroughly frightened—not with the prosaic fright that a man suffers in a war, but with a heady, bounding kind of fear that was hardly distinguishable from his general excitement: he was poised on a sort of emotional watershed from which, he felt, he might at any moment pass into delirious terror or into an ecstasy of joy. He knew now that he was not in a house, but in some moving vessel. It was clearly not a submarine: and the infinitesimal quivering of the metal did not suggest the motion of any wheeled vehicle. A ship then, he supposed, or some kind of airship . . . but there was an oddity in all his sensations for which neither supposition accounted. Puzzled, he sat down again on the bed, and stared at the portentous moon.

An airship, some kind of flying-machine . . . but why did the moon look so big? It was larger than he had thought at first. No moon could really be that size; and he realized now that he had known this from the first but had repressed the knowledge through terror. At the same moment a thought came into his head which stopped his breath—there could be no full moon at all that night. He remembered distinctly that he had walked from Nadderby in a moonless night. Even if the thin crescent of a new moon had escaped his notice, it could not have grown to this in a few hours. It could not have grown to this at all—this megalomaniac disk, far larger than the football he had at first compared it to, larger than a child's hoop, filling almost half the sky. And where was the old 'man in the moon'—the familiar face that had looked down on all the generations of men? The thing wasn't the Moon at all; and he felt his hair move on his scalp.

At that moment the sound of an opening door made him turn his head. An oblong of dazzling light appeared behind him and instantly vanished as the door closed again, having admitted the bulky form of a naked man whom Ransom recognized as Weston. No reproach, no demand for an explanation, rose to Ransom's lips or even to his mind; not with that monstrous orb above them. The mere presence of a human being, with its offer of at least some companionship, broke down the tension in which his nerves had long been resisting a bottomless dismay. He found, when he spoke, that he was sobbing.

'Weston! Weston!' he gasped. 'What is it? It's not the moon, not that size. It can't be, can it?'

'No,' replied Weston, 'it's the Earth.'

## Chapter 4

RANSOM'S LEGS failed him, and he must have sunk back upon the bed, but he only became aware of this many minutes later. At the moment he was unconscious of everything except his fear. He did not even know what he was afraid of: the fear itself possessed his whole mind, a formless, infinite misgiving. He did not lose consciousness, though he greatly wished that he might do so. Any change—death or sleep, or, best of all, a waking which should show all this for a dream —would have been inexpressibly welcome. None came. Instead, the lifelong self-control of social man, the virtues which are half hypocrisy or the hypocrisy which is half a virtue, came back to him and soon he found himself answering Weston in a voice not shamefully tremulous.

'Do you mean that?' he asked.

'Certainly.'

'Then where are we?'

'Standing out from Earth about eighty-five thousand miles.'

'You mean we're—in space.' Ransom uttered the word with difficulty as a frightened child speaks of ghosts or a frightened man of cancer.

Weston nodded.

'What for?' said Ransom. 'And what on earth have you kidnapped me for? And how have you done it?'

For a moment Weston seemed disposed to give no answer; then, as if on a second thought, he sat down on the bed beside Ransom and spoke as follows:

'I suppose it will save trouble if I deal with these questions at once, instead of leaving you to pester us with them every hour for the next month. As to how we do it—I suppose you mean how the space-ship works—there's no good your asking that. Unless you were one of the four or five real physicists now living you couldn't understand: and if there were any chance of your understanding you certainly wouldn't be told. If it makes you happy to repeat words that don't mean anything—which is, in fact, what unscientific people want when they ask for an explanation—you may say we work by exploiting the less observed properties of solar radiation. As to why we are here, we are on our way to Malacandra. . . .'

'Do you mean a star called Malacandra?'

'Even you can hardly suppose we are going out of the solar system. Malacandra is much nearer than that: we shall make it in about twenty-eight days.'

'There isn't a planet called Malacandra,' objected Ransom.

'I am giving it its real name, not the name invented by terrestrial astronomers,' said Weston.

'But surely this is nonsense,' said Ransom. 'How the deuce did you find out its real name, as you call it?'

'From the inhabitants.'

It took Ransom some time to digest this statement. 'Do you mean to tell me you claim to have been to this star before, or this planet, or whatever it is?'

'Yes.'

'You can't really ask me to believe that,' said Ransom. 'Damn it all, it's not an everyday affair. Why has no one heard of it? Why has it not been in all the papers?'

'Because we are not perfect idiots,' said Weston gruffly.

After a few moments' silence Ransom began again. 'Which planet is it in our terminology?' he asked.

'Once and for all,' said Weston, 'I am not going to tell you. If you know how to find out when we get there, you are welcome to do so: I don't think we have much to fear from your scientific attainments. In the meantime, there is no reason for you to know.'

'And you say this place is inhabited?' said Ransom.

Weston gave him a peculiar look and then nodded. The uneasiness which this produced in Ransom rapidly merged in an anger which he had almost lost sight of amidst the conflicting emotions that beset him.

'And what has all this to do with me?' he broke out. 'You have assaulted me, drugged me, and are apparently carrying me off as a prisoner in this infernal thing. What have I done to you? What do you say for yourself?'

'I might reply by asking you why you crept into my back-yard like a thief. If you had minded your own business you would not be here. As it is, I admit that we have had to infringe your rights. My only defence is that small claims must give way to great. As far as we know, we are doing what has never been done in the history of man, perhaps never in the history of the universe. We have learned how to jump off the speck of matter on which our species began; infinity, and therefore perhaps eternity, is being put into the hands of the human race. You cannot be so small-minded as to think that the rights or the life of an individual or of a million individuals are of the slightest importance in comparison with this.'

'I happen to disagree,' said Ransom, 'and I always have disagreed, even about vivisection. But you haven't answered my question. What do you want me for? What good am I to do you on this—on Malacandra.'

'That I don't know,' said Weston. 'It was no idea of ours. We are only obeying orders.'

'Whose?'

There was another pause. 'Come,' said Weston at last, 'there is really no use in continuing this cross-examination. You keep on asking me questions I can't answer: in some cases because I don't know the answers, in others because you wouldn't understand them. It will make things very much pleasanter during the voyage if you can only resign your mind to your fate and stop bothering yourself and us. It would be easier if your philosophy of life were not so insufferably narrow and individualistic. I had thought no one could fail to be inspired by the role you are being asked to play: that even a worm, if it could understand, would rise to the sacrifice. I mean, of course, the sacrifice of time and liberty, and some little risk. Don't misunderstand me.'

'Well,' said Ransom, 'you hold all the cards, and I must make the best of it. I consider *your* philosophy of life raving lunacy. I suppose all that stuff about infinity and eternity means that you think you are justified in doing anything— absolutely anything—here and now, on the off chance that some creatures or other descended from man as we know him may crawl about a few centuries longer in some part of the universe.'

'Yes—anything whatever,' returned the scientist sternly, 'and all educated opinion—for I do not call classics and history and such trash education—is entirely on my side. I am glad you raised the point, and I advise you to remember my answer. In the meantime, if you will follow me into the next room, we will have breakfast. Be careful how you get up: your weight here is hardly appreciable compared with your weight on Earth.'

Ransom rose and his captor opened the door. Instantly the room was flooded with a dazzling golden light which completely eclipsed the pale earthlight behind him.

'I will give you darkened glasses in a moment,' said Weston as he preceded him into the chamber whence the radiance was pouring. It seemed to Ransom that Weston went up a hill towards the doorway and disappeared suddenly downwards when he had passed it. When he followed—which he did with caution—he had the curious impression that he was walking up to the edge of a precipice: the new room beyond the doorway seemed to be built on its side so that its farther wall lay almost in the same plane as the floor of the room he was leaving. When, however, he ventured to put forward his foot, he found that the floor continued flush and as he entered the second room the walls suddenly righted themselves and the rounded ceiling was over his head. Looking back, he perceived that the bedroom in its turn was now heeling over —its roof a wall and one of its walls a roof.

'You will soon get used to it,' said Weston, following his gaze. 'The ship is roughly spherical, and now we are outside the gravitational field of the Earth "down" means—and feels —towards the centre of our own little metal world. This, of course, was foreseen and we built her accordingly. The core of the ship is a hollow globe—we keep our stores inside it— and the surface of that globe is the floor we are walking on. The cabins are arranged all round this, their walls supporting an outer globe which from our point of view is the roof. As the centre is always "down," the piece of floor you are standing on always feels flat or horizontal and the wall you are standing against always seems vertical. On the other hand, the globe of floor is so small that you can always see over the edge of it—over what would be the horizon if you were a flea—and then you see the floors and wall of the next cabin in a different plane. It is just the same on Earth, of course, only we are not big enough to see it.'

After this explanation he made arrangements in his precise, ungracious way for the comfort of his guest or prisoner.

Ransom, at his advice, removed all his clothes and substituted a little metal girdle hung with enormous weights to reduce, as far as possible, the unmanageable lightness of his body. He also assumed tinted glasses, and soon found himself seated opposite Weston at a small table laid for breakfast. He was both hungry and thirsty and eagerly attacked the meal which consisted of tinned meat, biscuit, butter and coffee.

But all these actions he had performed mechanically. Stripping, eating and drinking passed almost unnoticed, and all he ever remembered of his first meal in the space-ship was the tyranny of heat and light. Both were present in a degree which would have been intolerable on Earth, but each had a new quality. The light was paler than any light of comparable intensity that he had ever seen; it was not pure white but the palest of all imaginable golds, and it cast shadows as sharp as a floodlight. The heat, utterly free from moisture, seemed to knead and stroke the skin like a gigantic masseur: it produced no tendency to drowsiness: rather, intense alacrity. His headache was gone: he felt vigilant, courageous and magnanimous as he had seldom felt on Earth. Gradually he dared to raise his eyes to the skylight. Steel shutters were drawn across all but a chink of the glass, and that chink was covered with blinds of some heavy and dark material; but still it was too bright to look at.

'I always thought space was dark and cold,' he remarked vaguely.

'Forgotten the sun?' said Weston contemptuously.

Ransom went on eating for some time. Then he began, 'If it's like this in the early morning,' and stopped, warned by the expression on Weston's face. Awe fell upon him: there were no mornings here, no evenings, and no night—nothing but the changeless noon which had filled for centuries beyond history so many millions of cubic miles. He glanced at Weston again, but the latter held up his hand.

'Don't talk,' he said. 'We have discussed all that is necessary. The ship does not carry oxygen enough for any unnecessary exertion; not even for talking.'

Shortly afterwards he rose, without inviting the other to follow him, and left the room by one of the many doors which Ransom had not yet seen opened.

## Chapter 5

THE PERIOD spent in the space-ship ought to have been one of terror and anxiety for Ransom. He was separated by an astronomical distance from every member of the human race except two whom he had excellent reasons for distrusting. He was heading for an unknown destination, and was being brought thither for a purpose which his captors steadily refused to disclose. Devine and Weston relieved each other regularly in a room which Ransom was never allowed to enter and where he supposed the controls of their machine must be. Weston, during his watches off, was almost entirely silent. Devine was more loquacious and would often talk and guffaw with the prisoner until Weston rapped on the wall of the control-room and warned them not to waste air. But Devine was secretive after a certain point. He was quite ready to laugh at Weston's solemn scientific idealism. He didn't give a damn, he said, for the future of the species or the meeting of two worlds.

'There's more to Malacandra than that,' he would add with a wink. But when Ransom asked him what more, he would lapse into satire and make ironical remarks about the white man's burden and the blessings of civilization.

'It *is* inhabited, then?' Ransom would press.

'Ah—there's always a native question in these things,' Devine would answer. For the most part his conversation ran on the things he would do when he got back to Earth: ocean-going yachts, the most expensive women and a big place on the Riviera figured largely in his plans. 'I'm not running all these risks for fun.'

Direct questions about Ransom's own role were usually met with silence. Only once, in reply to such a question, Devine, who was then in Ransom's opinion very far from sober, admitted that they were rather 'handing him the baby.'

'But I'm sure,' he added, 'you'll live up to the old school tie.'

All this, as I have said, was sufficiently disquieting. The

odd thing was that it did not very greatly disquiet him. It is hard for a man to brood on the future when he is feeling so extremely well as Ransom now felt. There was an endless night on one side of the ship and an endless day on the other: each was marvellous and he moved from the one to the other at his will, delighted. In the nights, which he could create by turning the handle of a door, he lay for hours in contemplation of the skylight. The Earth's disk was nowhere to be seen; the stars, thick as daisies on an uncut lawn, reigned perpetually with no cloud, no moon, no sunrise to dispute their sway. There were planets of unbelievable majesty, and constellations undreamed of: there were celestial sapphires, rubies, emeralds and pin-pricks of burning gold; far out on the left of the picture hung a comet, tiny and remote: and between all and behind all, far more emphatic and palpable than it showed on Earth, the undimensioned, enigmatic blackness. The lights trembled: they seemed to grow brighter as he looked. Stretched naked on his bed, a second Danaë, he found it night by night more difficult to disbelieve in old astrology: almost he felt, wholly he imagined, 'sweet influence' pouring or even stabbing into his surrendered body. All was silence but for the irregular tinkling noises. He knew now that these were made by meteorites, small, drifting particles of the world-stuff that smote continually on their hollow drum of steel; and he guessed that at any moment they might meet something large enough to make meteorites of ship and all. But he could not fear. He now felt that Weston had justly called him little-minded in the moment of his first panic. The adventure was too high, its circumstance too solemn, for any emotion save a severe delight. But the days—that is, the hours spent in the sunward hemisphere of their microcosm—were the best of all. Often he rose after only a few hours' sleep to return, drawn by an irresistible attraction, to the regions of light; he could not cease to wonder at the noon which always awaited you however early you went to seek it. There, totally immersed in a bath of pure ethereal colour and of unrelenting though unwounding brightness, stretched his full length and with eyes half closed in the strange chariot that bore them, faintly quivering, through depth after depth of tranquillity far above the reach of night, he felt his body and mind daily rubbed and scoured and filled with new vitality. Weston, in one of his brief, reluctant answers, admitted a scientific basis for these sensations: they were receiving, he said, many rays that never penetrated the terrestrial atmosphere.

But Ransom, as time wore on, became aware of another and more spiritual cause for his progressive lightening and exultation of heart. A nightmare, long engendered in the modern mind by the mythology that follows in the wake of science, was falling off him. He had read of 'Space': at the back of his thinking for years had lurked the dismal fancy of the black, cold vacuity, the utter deadness, which was supposed to separate the worlds. He had not known how much it affected him till now—now that the very name 'Space' seemed a blasphemous libel for this empyrean ocean of radiance in which they swam. He could not call it 'dead'; he felt life pouring into him from it every moment. How indeed should it be otherwise, since out of this ocean the worlds and all their life had come? He had thought it barren: he saw now that it was the womb of worlds, whose blazing and innumerable offspring looked down nightly even upon the earth with so many eyes—and here, with how many more! No: Space was the wrong name. Older thinkers had been wiser when they named it simply the heavens—the heavens which declared the glory—the

'happy climes that ly
Where day never shuts his eye
Up in the broad fields of the sky.'

He quoted Milton's words to himself lovingly, at this time and often.

He did not, of course, spend all his time in basking. He explored the ship (so far as he was allowed), passing from room to room with those slow movements which Weston enjoined upon them lest exertion should overtax their supply of air. From the necessity of its shape, the space-ship contained a good many more chambers than were in regular use: but Ransom was also inclined to think that its owners— or at least Devine—intended these to be filled with cargo of some kind on the return voyage. He also became, by an insensible

process, the steward and cook of the company; partly because
he felt it natural to share the only labours he could share—
he was never allowed into the control-room—and partly in
order to anticipate a tendency which Weston showed to make
him a servant whether he would or no. He preferred to work
as a volunteer rather than in admitted slavery: and he liked
his own cooking a good deal more than that of his companions.

It was these duties that made him at first the unwilling,
and then the alarmed, hearer of a conversation which occurred
about a fortnight (he judged) after the beginning of their
voyage. He had washed up the remains of their evening
meal, basked in the sunlight, chatted with Devine—better
company than Weston, though in Ransom's opinion much
the more odious of the two—and retired to bed at his usual
time. He was a little restless, and after an hour or so it occurred to him that he had forgotten one or two small arrangements in the galley which would facilitate his work in the
morning. The galley opened off the saloon or day-room, and
its door was close to that of the control-room. He rose and
went there at once. His feet, like the rest of him, were bare.

The galley skylight was on the dark side of the ship, but
Ransom did not turn on the light. To leave the door ajar was
sufficient, as this admitted a stream of brilliant sunlight. As
everyone who has 'kept house' will understand, he found that
his preparations for the morning had been even more incom-
plete than he supposed. He did his work well, from practice,
and therefore quietly. He had just finished and was drying
his hands on the roller-towel behind the galley door when he
heard the door of the control-room open and saw the silhou-
ette of a man outside the galley—Devine's, he gathered.
Devine did not come forward into the saloon, but remained
standing and talking—apparently into the control-room. It
thus came about that while Ransom could hear distinctly
what Devine said he could not make out Weston's answers.

'I think it would be dam' silly,' said Devine. 'If you could
be sure of meeting the brutes where we alight there might be
something in it. But suppose we have to trek? All we'd gain
by your plan would be having to carry a drugged man and

his pack instead of letting a live man walk with us and do his share of the work.'

Weston apparently replied.

'But he *can't* find out,' returned Devine. 'Unless someone is fool enough to tell him. Anyway, even if he suspects, do you think a man like that would have the guts to run away on a strange planet? Without food? Without weapons? You'll find he'll eat out of your hand at the first sight of a *sorn.*'

Again Ransom heard the indistinct noise of Weston's voice.

'How should I know?' said Devine. 'It may be some sort of chief: much more likely a mumbo-jumbo.'

This time came a very short utterance from the control-room: apparently a question. Devine answered at once.

'It would explain why he was wanted.'

Weston asked him something more.

'Human sacrifice, I suppose. At least it wouldn't be human from *their* point of view; you know what I mean.'

Weston had a good deal to say this time, and it elicited Devine's characteristic chuckle.

'Quite, quite,' he said. 'It is understood that you are doing it all from the highest motives. So long as they lead to the same actions as *my* motives, you are quite welcome to them.'

Weston continued; and this time Devine seemed to interrupt him.

'You're not losing your own nerve, are you?' he said. He was then silent for some time, as if listening. Finally, he replied:

'If you're so fond of the brutes as that you'd better stay and interbreed—if they have sexes, which we don't yet know. Don't you worry. When the time comes for cleaning the place up we'll save one or two for you, and you can keep them as pets or vivisect them or sleep with them or all three—whichever way it takes you. . . . Yes, I know. Perfectly loathsome. I was only joking. Good night.'

A moment later Devine closed the door of the control-room, crossed the saloon and entered his own cabin. Ransom heard him bolt the door of it according to his invariable, though puzzling, custom. The tension with which he had been listening relaxed. He found that he had been holding his

breath, and breathed deeply again. Then cautiously he stepped
out into the saloon.

Though he knew that it would be prudent to return to his
bed as quickly as possible, he found himself standing still in
the now familiar glory of the light and viewing it with a new
and poignant emotion. Out of this heaven, these happy climes,
they were presently to descend—into *what*? *Sorns*, human
sacrifice, loathsome sexless monsters. What was a *sorn*? His
own role in the affair was now clear enough. Somebody or
something had sent for him. It could hardly be for him
personally. The somebody wanted a victim—any victim—
from Earth. He had been picked because Devine had done
the picking; he realized for the first time—in all circumstances
a late and startling discovery—that Devine had hated him
all these years as heartily as he hated Devine. But what was
a *sorn*? 'When he saw them he would eat out of Devine's
hands.' His mind, like so many minds of his generation, was
richly furnished with bogies. He had read his H. G. Wells
and others. His universe was peopled with horrors such as
ancient and mediæval mythology could hardly rival. No
insect-like, vermiculate or crustacean Abominable, no twitch-
ing feelers, rasping wings, slimy coils, curling tentacles, no
monstrous union of superhuman intelligence and insatiable
cruelty seemed to him anything but likely on an alien world.
The *sorns* would be . . . would be . . . he dared not think
what the *sorns* would be. And he was to be given to them.
Somehow this seemed more horrible than being caught by
them. Given, handed over, offered. He saw in imagination
various incompatible monstrosities—bulbous eyes, grinning
jaws, horns, stings, mandibles. Loathing of insects, loathing
of snakes, loathing of things that squashed and squelched, all
played their horrible symphonies over his nerves. But the
reality would be worse: it would be an extra-terrestrial Other-
ness—something one had never thought of, never could have
thought of. In that moment Ransom made a decision. He
could face death, but not the *sorns*. He must escape when
they got to Malacandra, if there were any possibility. Starva-
tion, or even to be chased by *sorns*, would be better than
being handed over. If escape were impossible, then it must
be suicide. Ransom was a pious man. He hoped he would

be forgiven. It was no more in his power, he thought, to decide otherwise than to grow a new limb. Without hesitation he stole back into the galley and secured the sharpest knife: henceforward he determined never to be parted from it.

Such was the exhaustion produced by terror that when he regained his bed he fell instantly into stupefied and dreamless sleep.

# Chapter 6

HE WOKE much refreshed, and even a little ashamed of his terror on the previous night. His situation was, no doubt, very serious: indeed the possibility of returning alive to Earth must be almost discounted. But death could be faced, and rational fear of death could be mastered. It was only the irrational, the biological, horror of monsters that was the real difficulty: and this he faced and came to terms with as well as he could while he lay in the sunlight after breakfast. He had the feeling that one sailing in the heavens, as he was doing, should not suffer abject dismay before any earthbound creature. He even reflected that the knife could pierce other flesh as well as his own. The bellicose mood was a very rare one with Ransom. Like many men of his own age, he rather underestimated than overestimated his own courage; the gap between boyhood's dreams and his actual experience of the War had been startling, and his subsequent view of his own unheroic qualities had perhaps swung too far in the opposite direction. He had some anxiety lest the firmness of his present mood should prove a short-lived illusion; but he must make the best of it.

As hour followed hour and waking followed sleep in their eternal day, he became aware of a gradual change. The temperature was slowly falling. They resumed clothes. Later, they added warm underclothes. Later still, an electric heater was turned on in the centre of the ship. And it became certain, too—though the phenomenon was hard to seize— that the light was less overwhelming than it had been at the beginning of the voyage. It became certain to the comparing intellect, but it was difficult to *feel* what was happening as a diminution of light and impossible to think of it as 'darkening' because, while the radiance changed in degree, its unearthly quality had remained exactly the same since the moment he first beheld it. It was not, like fading light upon the Earth, mixed with the increasing moisture and phantom colours of the air. You might halve its intensity, Ransom perceived, and the remaining half would still be what the whole had been—

merely less, not other. Halve it again, and the residue would still be the same. As long as it was at all, it would be itself—out even to that unimagined distance where its last force was spent. He tried to explain what he meant to Devine.

'Like thingummy's soap!' grinned Devine. 'Pure soap to the last bubble, eh?'

Shortly after this the even tenor of their life in the space-ship began to be disturbed. Weston explained that they would soon begin to feel the gravitational pull of Malacandra.

'That means,' he said, 'that it will not longer be "down" to the centre of the ship. It will be "down" towards Malacandra —which from our point of view will be under the control-room. As a consequence, the floors of most of the chambers will become wall or roof, and one of the walls a floor. You won't like it.'

The result of this announcement, so far as Ransom was concerned, was hours of heavy labour in which he worked shoulder to shoulder now with Devine and now with Weston as their alternating watches liberated them from the control-room. Water-tins, oxygen-cylinders, guns, ammunition and foodstuffs had all to be piled on the floors alongside the appropriate walls and lying on their sides so as to be upright when the new 'downwards' came into play. Long before the work was finished disturbing sensations began. At first Ransom supposed that it was the toil itself which so weighted his limbs: but rest did not alleviate the symptom, and it was explained to him that their bodies, in response to the planet that had caught them in its field, were actually gaining weight every minute and doubling in weight with every twenty-four hours. They had the experiences of a pregnant woman, but magnified almost beyond endurance.

At the same time their sense of direction—never very confident on the space-ship—became continuously confused. From any room on board, the next room's floor had always looked downhill and felt level: now it looked downhill and felt a little, a very little, downhill as well. One found oneself running as one entered it. A cushion flung aside on the floor of the saloon would be found hours later to have moved an inch or so towards the wall. All of them were afflicted with vomiting, headache and palpitations of the heart. The conditions grew worse hour by hour. Soon one could only grope and crawl from cabin to cabin. All sense of direction disappeared in a sickening confusion. Parts of the ship were definitely below in the sense that their floors were upside down and only a fly could walk on them: but no part seemed to Ransom to be indisputably the right way up. Sensations of intolerable height and of falling—utterly absent in the heavens —recurred constantly. Cooking, of course, had long since been abandoned. Food was snatched as best they could, and drinking presented great difficulties: you could never be sure that you were really holding your mouth below, rather than beside, the bottle. Weston grew grimmer and more silent than ever. Devine, a flask of spirits ever in his hand, flung out strange blasphemies and coprologies and cursed Weston for bringing them. Ransom ached, licked his dry lips, nursed his bruised limbs and prayed for the end.

A time came when one side of the sphere was unmistakably down. Clamped beds and tables hung useless and ridiculous on what was now wall or roof. What had been doors became trapdoors, opened with difficulty. Their bodies seemed made of lead. There was no more work to be done when Devine had set out the clothes—their Malacandrian clothes—from their bundles and squatted down on the end of the saloon (now its floor) to watch the thermometer. The clothes, Ransom noticed, included heavy woollen underwear, sheepskin jerkins, fur gloves and eared caps. Devine made no reply to his questions. He was engaged in studying the thermometer and in shouting down to Weston in the control-room.

'Slower, slower,' he kept shouting. 'Slower, you damned fool. You'll be in air in a minute or two.' Then sharply and angrily, 'Here! Let me get at it.'

Weston made no replies. It was unlike Devine to waste his advice: Ransom concluded that the man was almost out of his senses, whether with fear or excitement.

Suddenly the lights of the Universe seemed to be turned down. As if some demon had rubbed the heaven's face with a dirty sponge, the splendour in which they had lived for so long blenched to a pallid, cheerless and pitiable grey. It was impossible from where they sat to open the shutters or roll back the heavy blind. What had been a chariot gliding in the fields of heaven became a dark steel box dimly lighted by a slit of window, and falling. They were falling out of the heaven, into a world. Nothing in all his adventures bit so deeply into Ransom's mind as this. He wondered how he could ever have thought of planets, even of the Earth, as islands of life and reality floating in a deadly void. Now, with a certainty which never after deserted him, he saw the planets— the 'earths' he called them in his thought—as mere holes or gaps in the living heaven—excluded and rejected wastes of heavy matter and murky air, formed not by addition to, but by subtraction from, the surrounding brightness. And yet, he thought, beyond the solar system the brightness ends. Is that the real void, the real death? Unless . . . he groped for the idea . . . unless visible light is also a hole or gap, a mere diminution of something else. Something that is to bright unchanging heaven as heaven is to the dark, heavy earths. . . .

Things do not always happen as a man would expect. The moment of his arrival in an unknown world found Ransom wholly absorbed in a philosophical speculation.

## Chapter 7

'HAVING A DOZE?' said Devine. 'A bit blasé about new planets by now?'

'Can you see anything?' interrupted Weston.

'I can't manage the shutters, damn them,' returned Devine. 'We may as well get to the manhole.'

Ransom awoke from his brown study. The two partners were working together close beside him in the semi-darkness. He was cold and his body, though in fact much lighter than on Earth, still felt intolerably heavy. But a vivid sense of his situation returned to him; some fear, but more curiosity. It might mean death, but what a scaffold! Already cold air was coming in from without, and light. He moved his head impatiently to catch some glimpse between the labouring shoulders of the two men. A moment later the last nut was unscrewed. He was looking out through the manhole.

Naturally enough all he saw was the ground—a circle of pale pink, almost of white: whether very close and short vegetation or very wrinkled and granulated rock or soil he could not say. Instantly the dark shape of Devine filled the aperture, and Ransom had time to notice that he had a revolver in his hand—'For me or for *sorns* or for both?' he wondered.

'You next,' said Weston curtly.

Ransom took a deep breath and his hand went to the knife beneath his belt. Then he got his head and shoulders through the manhole, his two hands on the soil of Malacandra. The pink stuff was soft and faintly resilient, like india-rubber; clearly vegetation. Instantly Ransom looked up. He saw a pale blue sky—a fine winter-morning sky it would have been on Earth—a great billowy cumular mass of rose-colour lower down which he took for a cloud, and then—

'Get out,' said Weston from behind him.

He scrambled through and rose to his feet. The air was cold but not bitterly so, and it seemed a little rough at the back of his throat. He gazed about him, and the very intensity

41

of his desire to take in the new world at a glance defeated itself. He saw nothing but colours—colours that refused to form themselves into things. Moreover, he knew nothing yet well enough to see it: you cannot see things till you know roughly what they are. His first impression was of a bright, pale world—a water-colour world out of child's paint-box; a moment later he recognized the flat belt of light blue as a sheet of water, or of something like water, which came nearly to his feet. They were on the shore of a lake or river.

'Now then,' said Weston, brushing past him. He turned and saw to his surprise a quite recognizable object in the immediate foreground—a hut of unmistakably terrestrial pattern though built of strange materials.

'They're human,' he gasped. 'They build houses?'

'*We* do,' said Devine. 'Guess again,' and, producing a key from his pocket, proceeded to unlock a very ordinary padlock on the door of the hut. With a not very clearly defined feeling of disappointment or relief Ransom realized that his captors were merely returning to their own camp. They behaved as one might have expected. They walked into the hut, let down the slats which served for windows, sniffed the close air, expressed surprise that they had left it so dirty, and presently re-emerged.

'We'd better see about the stores,' said Weston.

Ransom soon realized that he was to have little leisure for observation and no opportunity of escape. The monotonous work of transferring food, clothes, weapons and many unidentifiable packages from the ship to the hut kept him vigorously occupied for the next hour or so, and in the closest contact with his kidnappers. But something he learned. Before anything else he learned that Malacandra was beautiful; and he even reflected how odd it was that this possibility had never entered into his speculations about it. The same peculiar twist of imagination which led him to people the universe with monsters had somehow taught him to expect nothing on a strange planet except rocky desolation or else a network of nightmare machines. He could not say why, now that he came to think of it. He also discovered that the blue water surrounded them on at least three sides: his view in the fourth direction was blotted out by the vast steel football in which they had come. The hut, in fact, was built either on the point of a peninsula or on the end of an island. He also came little by little to the conclusion that the water was not merely blue in certain lights like terrestrial water but 'really' blue. There was something about its behaviour under the very gentle breeze which puzzled him—something wrong or unnatural about the waves. For one thing, they were too big for such a wind, but that was not the whole secret. They reminded him somehow of the water that he had seen shooting up under the impact of shells in pictures of naval battles. Then suddenly realization came to him: they were the wrong shape, out of drawing, far too high for their length, too narrow at the base, too steep in the sides. He was reminded of something he had read in one of those modern poets about a sea rising in 'turreted walls.'

'Catch!' shouted Devine. Ransom caught and hurled the parcel on to Weston at the hut door.

On one side the water extended a long way—about a quarter of a mile, he thought, but perspective was still difficult in the strange world. On the others side it was much narrower, not wider than fifteen feet perhaps, and seemed to be flowing over a shallow—broken and swirling water that made a softer and more hissing sound than water on Earth; and where it washed the hither bank—the pinkish-white vegetation went down to the very brink—there was a bubbling and sparkling which suggested effervescence. He tried hard, in such stolen glances as the work allowed him, to make out something of the farther shore. A mass of something purple, so huge that he took it for a heather-covered mountain, was his first impression: on the other side, beyond the larger water, there was something of the same kind. But there, he could see over the top of it. Beyond were strange upright shapes of whitish green: too jagged and irregular for buildings, too thin and steep for mountains. Beyond and above these again was the rose-coloured cloud-like mass. It might really be a cloud, but it was very solid-looking and did not seem to have moved since he first set eyes on it from the manhole. It looked like the top of a gigantic red cauliflower—or like a huge bowl of red soapsuds—and it was exquisitely beautiful in tint and shape.

Baffled by this, he turned his attention to the nearer shore beyond the shallows. The purple mass looked for a moment like a plump of organ-pipes, then like a stack of rolls of cloth set up on end, then like a forest of gigantic umbrellas blown inside out. It was in faint motion. Suddenly his eyes mastered the object. The purple stuff was vegetation: more precisely it was vegetables, vegetables about twice the height of English elms, but apparently soft and flimsy. The stalks— one could hardly call them trunks—rose smooth and round, and surprisingly thin, for about forty feet: above that, the huge plants opened into a sheaf-like development, not of branches but of leaves, leaves large as lifeboats but nearly transparent. The whole thing corresponded roughly to his idea of a submarine forest: the plants, at once so large and so frail, seemed to need water to support them, and he wondered that they could hang in the air. Lower down, between the stems, he saw the vivid purple twilight, mottled with paler sunshine, which made up the internal scenery of the wood.

'Time for lunch,' said Devine suddenly. Ransom straightened his back: in spite of the thinness and coldness of the air, his forehead was moist. They had been working hard and he was short of breath. Weston appeared from the door of the hut and muttered something about 'finishing first.' Devine, however, overruled him. A tin of beef and some biscuits were produced, and the men sat down on the various boxes which were still plentifully littered between the space-ship and the hut. Some whiskey—again at Devine's suggestion and against Weston's advice—was poured into the tin cups and mixed with water; the latter, Ransom noticed, was drawn from their own water-tins and not from the blue lakes.

As often happens, the cessation of bodily activity drew Ransom's attention to the excitement under which he had been labouring ever since their landing. Eating seemed almost out of the question. Mindful, however, of a possible dash for liberty, he forced himself to eat very much more than usual, and appetite returned as he ate. He devoured all that he could lay hands on either of food or drink: and the taste of that first meal was ever after associated in his mind with the first unearthly strangeness (never fully recaptured) of the bright, still, sparkling, unintelligible landscape—with needling shapes of pale green, thousands of feet high, with sheets of dazzling blue soda-water, and acres of rose-red soapsuds. He was a little afraid that his companions might notice, and suspect, his new achievements as a trencherman; but their attention was otherwise engaged. Their eyes never ceased roving the landscape; they spoke abstractedly and often changed position, and were ever looking over their shoulders. Ransom was just finishing his protracted meal when he saw Devine stiffen like a dog, and lay his hand in silence on Weston's shoulder. Both nodded. They rose. Ransom, gulping down the last of his whiskey, rose too. He found himself between his two captors. Both revolvers were out. They were edging him to the shore of the narrow water, and they were looking and pointing across it.

At first he could not see clearly what they were pointing at. There seemed to be some paler and slenderer plants than he had noticed before amongst the purple ones: he hardly attended to them, for his eyes were busy searching the ground— so obsessed was he with the reptile fears and insect fears of modern imagining. It was the reflections of the new white objects in the water than sent his eyes back to them: long, streaky, white reflections motionless in the running water— four or five, no, to be precise, six of them. He looked up. Six white things *were* standing there. Spindly and flimsy things, twice or three times the height of a man. His first idea was that they were images of men, the work of savage artists; he had seen things like them in books of archæology. But what could they be made of, and how could they stand?—so crazily thin and elongated in the leg, so top-heavily pouted in the chest, such stalky, flexible-looking distortions of earthly bipeds . . . like something seen in one of those comic mirrors. They were certainly not made of stone or metal, for now they seemed to sway a little as he watched; now with a shock that chased the blood from his cheeks he saw that they were alive, that they were moving, that they were coming at him. He had a momentary, scared glimpse of their faces, thin and unnaturally long, with long, drooping noses and drooping mouths of half-spectral, half-idiotic solemnity. Then he turned wildly to fly and found himself gripped by Devine.

'Let me go,' he cried.

'Don't be a fool,' hissed Devine, offering the muzzle of his pistol. Then, as they struggled, one of the things sent its voice across the water to them: an enormous horn-like voice far above their heads.

'They want us to go across,' said Weston.

Both the men were forcing him to the water's edge. He planted his feet, bent his back and resisted donkey-fashion. Now the other two were both in the water, pulling him, and he was still on the land. He found that he was screaming. Suddenly a second, much louder and less articulate noise broke from the creatures on the far bank. Weston shouted too, relaxed his grip on Ransom and suddenly fired his revolver not across the water but up it. Ransom saw why at the same moment.

A line of foam like the track of a torpedo was speeding towards them, and in the midst of it some large, shining beast. Devine shrieked a curse, slipped and collapsed into the water. Ransom saw a snapping jaw between them, and heard the deafening noise of Weston's revolver again and again beside him and, almost as loud, the clamour of the monsters on the far bank, who seemed to be taking the water too. He had had no need to make a decision. The moment he was free he had found himself automatically darting behind his captors, then behind the space-ship and on as fast as his legs could carry him into the utterly unknown beyond it. As he rounded the metal sphere a wild confusion of blue, purple and red met his eyes. He did not slacken his pace for a moment's inspection. He found himself splashing through water and crying out not with pain but with surprise because the water was warm. In less than a minute he was climbing out on to dry land again. He was running up a steep incline. And now he was running through purple shadow between the stems of another forest of the huge plants.

# Chapter 8

A MONTH OF INACTIVITY, a heavy meal and an unknown world do not help a man to run. Half an hour later, Ransom was walking, not running, through the forest, with a hand pressed to his aching side and his ears strained for any noise of pursuit. The clamour of revolver-shots and voices behind him (not all human voices) had been succeeded first by rifle-shots and calls at long intervals and then by utter silence. As far as eye could reach he saw nothing but the stems of the great plants about him receding in the violet shade, and far overhead the multiple transparency of huge leaves filtering the sunshine to the solemn splendour of twilight in which he walked. Whenever he felt able he ran again; the ground continued soft and springy, covered with the same resilient weed which was the first thing his hands had touched in Malacandra. Once or twice a small red creature scuttled across his path, but otherwise there seemed to be no life stirring in the wood; nothing to fear—except the fact of wandering unprovisioned and alone in a forest of unknown vegetation thousands or millions of miles beyond the reach or knowledge of man.

But Ransom was thinking of *sorns*—for doubtless those were the *sorns*, those creatures they had tried to give him to. They were quite unlike the horrors his imagination had conjured up, and for that reason had taken him off his guard. They appealed away from the Wellsian fantasies to an earlier, almost an infantile, complex of fears. Giants—ogres—ghosts —skeletons: those were its key words. Spooks on stilts, he said to himself; surrealistic bogy-men with their long faces. At the same time, the disabling panic of the first moments was ebbing away from him. The idea of suicide was now far from his mind; instead, he was determined to back his luck to the end. He prayed, and he felt his knife. He felt a strange emotion of confidence and affection towards himself—he checked himself on the point of saying, 'We'll stick to one another.'

The ground became worse and interrupted his meditation. He had been going gently upwards for some hours with steeper ground on his right, apparently half scaling, half skirting a hill. His path now began to cross a number of ridges, spurs doubtless of the higher ground on the right. He did not know why he should cross them, but for some reason he did; possibly a vague memory of earthly geography suggested that the lower ground would open out to bare places between wood and water where *sorns* would be more likely to catch him. As he continued crossing ridges and gullies he was struck with their extreme steepness; but somehow they were not very difficult to cross. He noticed, too, that even the smallest hummocks of earth were of an unearthly shape—too narrow, too pointed at the top and too small at the base. He remembered that the waves on the blue lakes had displayed a similar oddity. And glancing up at the purple leaves he saw the same theme of perpendicularity—the same rush to the sky—repeated there. They did not tip over at the ends; vast as they were, air was sufficient to support them so that the long aisles of the forest all rose to a kind of fan tracery. And the *sorns*, likewise—he shuddered as he thought it—they too were madly elongated.

He had sufficient science to guess that he must be on a world lighter than the Earth, where less strength was needed and nature was set free to follow her skyward impulse on a superterrestrial scale. This set him wondering where he was. He could not remember whether Venus was larger or smaller than Earth, and he had an idea that she would be hotter than this. Perhaps he was on Mars; perhaps even on the Moon. The latter he at first rejected on the ground that, if it were so, he ought to have seen the Earth in the sky when they landed; but later he remembered having been told that one face of the Moon was always turned away from the Earth. For all he knew he was wandering on the Moon's outer side; and, irrationally enough, this idea brought about him a bleaker sense of desolation than he had yet felt.

Many of the gullies which he crossed now carried streams, blue hissing streams, all hastening to the lower ground on his left. Like the lake they were warm, and the air was warm above them, so that as he climbed down and up the sides of

the gullies he was continually changing temperatures. It was
the contrast, as he crested the farther bank of one such small
ravine, which first drew his attention to the growing chilliness
of the forest; and as he looked about him he became certain
that the light was failing too. He had not taken night into his
calculations. He had no means of guessing what night might
be on Malacandra. As he stood gazing into the deepening
gloom a sigh of cold wind crept through the purple stems and
set them all swaying, reavealing once again the startling contrast between their size and their apparent flexibility and
lightness. Hunger and weariness, long kept at bay by the
mingled fear and wonder of his situation, smote him suddenly.
He shivered and forced himself to proceed. The wind increased. The mighty leaves danced and dipped above his
head, admitting glimpses of a pale and then a paler sky; and
then, discomfortingly, of a sky with one or two stars in it. The
wood was no longer silent. His eyes darted hither and thither
in search of an approaching enemy and discovered only how
quickly the darkness grew upon him. He welcomed the
streams now for their warmth.

It was this that first suggested to him a possible protection
against the increasing cold. There was really no use in going
farther; for all he knew he might as well be walking towards
danger as away from it. All was danger; he was no safer
travelling than resting. Beside some stream it might be warm
enough to lie. He shuffled on to find another gully, and went
so far that he began to think he had got out of the region of
them. He had almost determined to turn back when the
ground began falling steeply; he slipped, recovered and found
himself on the bank of a torrent. The trees—for as 'trees' he
could not help regarding them—did not quite meet overhead,
and the water itself seemed to have some faintly phosphor-
escent quality, so that it was lighter here. The fall from right
to left was steep. Guided by some vague picnicker's hankering
for a 'better' place, he went a few yards upstream. The valley
grew steeper, and he came to a little cataract. He noticed dully
that the water seemed to be descending a little too slowly for the
incline, but he was too tired to speculate about it. The water
was apparently hotter than that of the lake—perhaps nearer
its subterranean source of heat. What he really wanted to

know was whether he dared drink it. He was very thirsty by now; but it looked very poisonous, very unwatery. He would try not to drink it; perhaps he was so tired that thirst would let him sleep. He sank on his knees and bathed his hands in the warm torrent; then he rolled over in a hollow close beside the fall, and yawned.

The sound of his own voice yawning—the old sound heard in night-nurseries, school dormitories and in so many bedrooms—liberated a flood of self-pity. He drew his knees up and hugged himself; he felt a sort of physical, almost a filial, love for his own body. He put his wrist-watch to his ear and found that it had stopped. He wound it. Muttering, half whimpering to himself, he thought of men going to bed on the far-distant planet Earth—men in clubs, and liners, and hotels, married men, and small children who slept with nurses in the room, and warm, tobacco-smelling men tumbled together in forecastles and dug-outs. The tendency to talk to himself was irresistible . . . 'We'll look after you, Ransom . . . we'll stick together, old man.' It occurred to him that one of those creatures with snapping jaws might live in the stream. 'You're quite right, Ransom,' he answered mumblingly. 'It's not a safe place to spend the night. We'll just rest a bit till you feel better, then we'll go on again. Not now. Presently.'

## Chapter 9

IT WAS THIRST that woke him. He had slept warm, though his clothes were damp, and found himself lying in sunlight, the blue waterfall at his side dancing and coruscating with every transparent shade in the whole gamut of blue and flinging strange lights far up to the underside of the forest leaves. The realization of his position, as it rolled heavily back upon consciousness, was unbearable. If only he hadn't lost his nerve the *sorns* would have killed him by now. Then he remembered with inexpressible relief that there was a man wandering in the wood—poor devil—he'd be glad to see him. He would come up to him and say, 'Hullo, Ransom,'—he stopped, puzzled. No, it was only himself: it *was* Ransom. Or was he? Who was the man whom he had led to a hot stream and tucked up in bed, telling him not to drink the strange water? Obviously some new-comer who didn't know the place as well as he. But whatever Ransom had told him, he was going to drink now. He lay down on the bank and plunged his face in the warm rushing liquid. It was good to drink. It had a strong mineral flavour, but it was very good. He drank again and found himself greatly refreshed and steadied. All that about the other Ransom was nonsense. He was quite aware of the danger of madness, and applied himself vigorously to his devotions and his toilet. Not that madness mattered much. Perhaps he was mad already, and not really on Malacandra but safe in bed in an English asylum. If only it might be so! He would ask Ransom—curse it! there his mind went playing the same trick again. He rose and began walking briskly away.

The delusions recurred every few minutes as long as this stage of his journey lasted. He learned to stand still mentally, as it were, and let them roll over his mind. It was no good bothering about them. When they were gone you could resume sanity again. Far more important was the problem of food. He tried one of the 'trees' with his knife. As he expected, it was toughly soft like a vegetable, not hard like wood. He cut a little piece out of it, and under this operation the whole gigantic organism vibrated to its top—it was like being able to shake the mast of a full-rigged ship with one hand. When he put it in his mouth he found it almost tasteless but by no means disagreeable, and for some minutes he munched away contentedly. But he made no progress. The stuff was quite unswallowable and could only be used as a chewing-gum. As such he used it, and after it many other pieces; not without some comfort.

It was impossible to continue yesterday's flight as a flight— inevitably it degenerated into an endless ramble, vaguely motivated by the search for food. The search was necessarily vague, since he did not know whether Malacandra held food for him nor how to recognize it if it did. He had one bad fright in the course of the morning, when, passing through a somewhat more open glade, he became aware first of a huge, yellow object, then of two, and then of an indefinite multitude coming towards him. Before he could fly he found himself in the midst of a herd of enormous pale furry creatures more like giraffes than anything else he could think of, except that they could and did raise themselves on their hind legs and even progress several paces in that position. They were slenderer, and very much higher, than giraffes, and were eating the leaves off the tops of the purple plants. They saw him and stared at him with their big liquid eyes, snorting in *basso profondissimo*, but had apparently no hostile intentions. Their appetite was voracious. In five minutes they had mutilated the tops of a few hundred 'trees' and admitted a new flood of sunlight into the forest. Then they passed on.

This episode had an infinitely comforting effect on Ransom. The planet was not, as he had begun to fear, lifeless except for *sorns*. Here was a very presentable sort of animal, an animal which man could probably tame, and whose food man could possibly share. If only it were possible to climb the 'trees'! He was staring about him with some idea of attempting this feat, when he noticed that the devastation wrought by the leaf-eating animals had opened a vista overhead beyond the plant-tops to a collection of the same greenish-white objects which he had seen across the lake at their first landing.

This time they were much closer. They were enormously high, so that he had to throw back his head to see the top of them. They were something like pylons in shape, but solid; irregular in height and grouped in an apparently haphazard and disorderly fashion. Some ended in points that looked from where he stood as sharp as needles, while others, after narrowing towards the summit, expanded again into knobs or platforms that seemed to his terrestrial eyes ready to fall at any moment. He noticed that the sides were rougher and more seamed with fissures than he had realized at first, and between two of them he saw a motionless line of twisting blue brightness—obviously a distant fall of water. It was this which finally convinced him that the things, in spite of their improbable shape, were mountains; and with that discovery the mere oddity of the prospect was swallowed up in the fantastic sublime. Here, he understood, was the full statement of that *perpendicular* theme which beast and plant and earth all played on Malacandra—here in this riot of rock, leaping and surging skyward like solid jets from some rock-fountain, and hanging by their own lightness in the air, so shaped, so elongated, that all terrestrial mountains must ever after seem to him to be mountains lying on their sides. He felt a lift and lightening at the heart.

But the next moment his heart stood still. Against the pallid background of the mountains and quite close to him—for the mountains themselves seemed but a quarter of a mile away —a moving shape appeared. He recognized it instantly as it moved slowly (and, he thought, stealthily) between two of the denuded plant-tops—the giant stature, the cadaverous leanness, the long, drooping, wizard-like profile of a *sorn*. The head appeared to be narrow and conical; the hands or paws with which it parted the stems before it as it moved were thin, mobile, spidery and almost transparent. He felt an immediate certainty that it was looking for him. All this he took in in an infinitesimal time. The ineffaceable image was hardly stamped on his brain before he was running as hard as he could into the thickest of the forest.

He had no plan save to put as many miles as he could between himself and the *sorn*. He prayed fervently that there might be only one; perhaps the wood was full of them—perhaps they had the intelligence to make a circle round him. No matter—there was nothing for it now but sheer running, running knife in hand. The fear had all gone into action; emotionally he was cool and alert, and ready—as ready as he ever would be—for the last trial. His flight led him downhill at an ever-increasing speed; soon the incline was so steep that if his body had had terrestrial gravity he would have been compelled to take to his hands and knees and clamber down. Then he saw something gleaming ahead of him. A minute later he had emerged from the wood altogether; he was standing, blinking in the light of sun and water, on the shore of a broad river, and looking out on a flat landscape of intermingled river, lake, island and promontory—the same sort of country on which his eyes had first rested in Malacandra.

There was no sound of pursuit. Ransom dropped down on his stomach and drank, cursing a world where *cold* water appeared to be unobtainable. Then he lay still to listen and to recover his breath. His eyes were upon the blue water. It was agitated. Circles shuddered and bubbles danced ten yards away from his face. Suddenly the water heaved and a round, shining, black thing like a cannon-ball came into sight. Then he saw eyes and mouth—a puffing mouth bearded with bubbles. More of the thing came up out of the water. It was gleaming black. Finally it splashed and wallowed to the shore and rose, steaming, on its hind legs—six or seven feet high and too thin for its height, like everything in Malacandra. It had a coat of thick black hair, lucid as seal-skin, very short legs with webbed feet, a broad beaver-like or fish-like tail, strong forelimbs with webbed claws or fingers, and some complication half-way up the belly which Ransom took to be its genitals. It was something like a penguin, something like an otter, something like a seal; the slenderness and flexibility of the body suggested a giant stoat. The great round head, heavily whiskered, was mainly responsible for the suggestion of seal; but it was higher in the forehead than a seal's and the mouth was smaller.

There comes a point at which the actions of fear and precaution are purely conventional, no longer felt as terror or hope by the fugitive. Ransom lay perfectly still, pressing his body as well down into the weed as he could, in obedience to a wholly theoretical idea that he might thus pass unobserved. He felt little emotion. He noted in a dry, objective way that this was apparently to be the end of his story—caught between a *sorn* from the land and a big, black animal from the water. He had, it is true, a vague notion that the jaws and mouth of the beast were not those of a carnivore; but he knew that he was too ignorant of zoology to do more than guess.

Then something happened which completely altered his state of mind. The creature, which was still steaming and shaking itself on the back and had obviously not seen him, opened its mouth and began to make noises. This in itself was not remarkable; but a lifetime of linguistic study assured Ransom almost at once that these were articulate noises. The creature was *talking*. It had a language. If you are not yourself a philologist, I am afraid you must take on trust the prodigious emotional consequences of this realization in Ransom's mind. A new world he had already seen—but a new, an extra-terrestrial, a non-human language was a different matter. Somehow he had not thought of this in connection with the *sorns;* now, it flashed upon him like a revelation. The love of knowledge is a kind of madness. In the fraction of a second which it took Ransom to decide that the creature was really talking, and while he still knew that he might be facing instant death, his imagination had leaped over every fear and hope and probability of his situation to follow the dazzling project of making a Malacandrian grammar. *An Introduction to the Malacandrian language—The Lunar verb—A Concise Martian-English Dictionary* . . . the titles flitted through his mind. And what might one not discover from the speech of a non-human race? The very form of language itself, the principle behind all possible languages, might fall into his hands. Unconsciously he raised himself on his elbow and stared at the black beast. It became silent. The huge bullet head swung round and lustrous amber eyes fixed him. There was no wind on the lake or in the wood. Minute after minute in utter silence the representatives of two so far-divided species stared each into the other's face.

Ransom rose to his knees. The creature leaped back, watching him intently, and they became motionless again. Then it came a pace nearer, and Ransom jumped up and retreated, but not far; curiosity held him. He summoned up his courage and advanced, holding out his hand; the beast misunderstood the gesture. It backed into the shallows of the lake and he

could see the muscles tightened under its sleek pelt, ready for
sudden movement. But there it stopped; it, too, was in the grip
of curiosity. Neither dared let the other approach, yet each
repeatedly felt the impulse to do so himself, and yielded to it.
It was foolish, frightening, ecstatic and unbearable all in one
moment. It was more than curiosity. It was like a courtship—
like the meeting of the first man and the first woman in the
world; it was like something beyond that; so natural is the contact of sexes, so limited the strangeness, so shallow the reti-
cence, so mild the repugnance to be overcome, compared with
the first tingling intercourse of two different, but rational,
species.

The creature suddenly turned and began walking away. A
disappointment like despair smote Ransom.

'Come back,' he shouted in English. The thing turned,
spread out its arms and spoke again in its unintelligible language; then it resumed its progress. It had not gone more than
twenty yards away when Ransom saw it stoop down and pick
something up. It returned. In its hand (he was already thinking of its webbed forepaw as a hand) it was carrying what
appeared to be a shell—the shell of some oyster-like creature,
but rounder and more deeply domed. It dipped the shell in
the lake and raised it full of water. Then it held the shell to its
own middle and seemed to be pouring something into the
water. Ransom thought with disgust that it was urinating in
the shell. Then he realized that the protuberances on the creature's belly were not genital organs nor organs at all; it was
wearing a kind of girdle hung with various pouch-like objects,
and it was adding a few drops of liquid from one of these to
the water in the shell. This done it raised the shell to its black
lips and drank—not throwing back its head like a man but
bowing it and sucking like a horse. When it had finished it re-
filled the shell and once again added a few drops from the
receptacle—it seemed to be some kind of skin bottle—at its
waist. Supporting the shell in its two arms, it extended them
towards Ransom. The intention was unmistakable. Hesitantly,
almost shyly, he advanced and took the cup. His finger-tips
touched the webbed membrane of the creature's paws and an
indescribable thrill of mingled attraction and repulsion ran
through him; then he drank. Whatever had been added to the

water was plainly alcoholic; he had never enjoyed a drink so much.

'Thank you,' he said in English. 'Thank you very much.'

The creature struck itself on the chest and made a noise. Ransom did not at first realize what it meant. Then he saw that it was trying to teach him its name—presumably the name of the species.

'*Hross*,' it said, '*Hross*,' and flapped itself.

'*Hross*,' repeated Ransom, and pointed at it; then 'Man,' and struck his own chest.

'*Hmā—hmā—hmān*,' imitated the *hross*. It picked up a handful of earth, where earth appeared between weed and water at the bank of the lake.

'*Handra*,' it said. Ransom repeated the word. Then an idea occurred to him.

'*Malacandra?*' he said in an inquiring voice. The *hross* rolled its eyes and waved its arms, obviously in an effort to indicate the whole landscape. Ransom was getting on well. *Handra* was earth the element; *Malac-andra* the 'earth' or planet as a whole. Soon he would find out what *Malac* meant. In the meantime 'H disappears after C' he noted, and made his first step in Malacandrian phonetics. The *hross* was now trying to teach him the meaning of *handramit*. He recognized the root *handra-* again (and noted 'They have suffixes as well as prefixes'), but this time he could make nothing of the *hross's* gestures, and remained ignorant what a *handramit* might be. He took the initiative by opening his mouth, pointing to it and going through the pantomine of eating. The Malacandrian word for *food* or *eat* which he got in return proved to contain consonants unreproducible by a human mouth, and Ransom, continuing the pantomine, tried to explain that his interest was practical as well as philological. The *hross* understood him, though he took some time to understand from its gestures that it was inviting him to follow it. In the end, he did so.

It took him only as far as where it had got the shell, and here, to his not very reasonable astonishment, Ransom found that a kind of boat was moored. Man-like, when he saw the artifact he felt more certain of the *hross's* rationality. He even valued the creature the more because the boat, allowing for the usual Malacandrian height and flimsiness, was really very like an earthly boat; only later did he set himself the question, 'What else could a boat be like?' The *hross* produced an oval platter of some tough but slightly flexible material, covered it with strips of spongy, orange-coloured substance and gave it to Ransom. He cut a convenient length off with his knife and began to eat; doubtfully at first and then ravenously. It had a bean-like taste but sweeter; good enough for a starving man. Then, as his hunger ebbed, the sense of his situation returned with dismaying force. The huge, seal-like creature seated beside him became unbearably ominous. It seemed friendly; but it was very big, very black, and he knew nothing at all about it. What were its relations to the *sorns?* And was it really as rational as it appeared?

It was only many days later that Ransom discovered how to deal with these sudden losses of confidence. They arose when the rationality of the *hross* tempted you to think of it as a man. Then it became abominable—a man seven feet high, with a snaky body, covered, face and all, with thick black animal hair, and whiskered like a cat. But starting from the other end you had an animal with everything an animal ought to have—glossy coat, liquid eye, sweet breath and whitest teeth—and added to all these, as though Paradise had never been lost and earliest dreams were true, the charm of speech and reason. Nothing could be more disgusting than the one impression; nothing more delightful than the other. It all depended on the point of view.

## Chapter 10

WHEN RANSOM HAD finished his meal and drunk again of the strong waters of Malacandra, his host rose and entered the boat. He did this head-first like an animal, his sinuous body allowing him to rest his hands on the bottom of the boat while his feet were still planted on the land. He completed the operation by flinging rump, tail and hind legs all together about five feet into the air and then whisking them neatly on board with an agility which would have been quite impossible to an animal of his bulk on Earth.

Having got into the boat, he proceeded to get out again and then pointed to it. Ransom understood that he was being invited to follow his example. The question which he wanted to ask above all others could not, of course, be put. Were the *hrossa* (he discovered later that this was the plural of *hross*) the dominant species on Malacandra, and the *sorns*, despite their more man-like shape, merely a semi-intelligent kind of cattle? Fervently he hoped that it might be so. On the other hand, the *hrossa* might be the domestic animals of the *sorns*, in which case the latter would be superintelligent. His whole imaginative training somehow encouraged him to associate superhuman intelligence with monstrosity of form and ruthlessness of will. To step on board the *hross's* boat might mean surrendering himself to *sorns* at the other end of the journey. On the other hand, the *hross's* invitation might be a golden opportunity of leaving the *sorn*-haunted forests for ever. And by this time the *hross* itself was becoming puzzled at his apparent inability to understand it. The urgency of its signs finally determined him. The thought of parting from the *hross* could not be seriously entertained; its animality shocked him in a dozen ways, but his longing to learn its language, and, deeper still, the shy, ineluctable fascination of unlike for unlike, the sense that the key to prodigious adventure was being put in his hands—all this had really attached him to it by bonds stronger than he knew. He stepped into the boat.

The boat was without seats. It had a very high prow, an

enormous expanse of free-board, and what seemed to Ransom an impossibly shallow draught. Indeed, very little of it even rested on the water; he was reminded of a modern European speed-boat. It was moored by something that looked at first like rope; but the *hross* cast off not by untying but by simply pulling the apparent rope in two as one might pull in two a piece of soft toffee or a roll of plasticine. It then squatted down on its rump in the stern-sheets and took up a paddle —a paddle of such enormous blade that Ransom wondered how the creature could wield it, till he again remembered how light a planet they were on. The length of the *hross's* body enabled him to work freely in the squatting position despite the high gunwale. It paddled quickly.

For the first few minutes they passed between banks wooded with the purple trees, upon a waterway not more than a hundred yards in width. Then they doubled a promontory, and Ransom saw that they were emerging on to a much larger sheet of water—a great lake, almost a sea. The *hross,* now taking great care and often changing direction and looking about it, paddled well out from the shore. The dazzling blue expanse grew moment by moment wider around them; Ransom could not look steadily at it. The warmth from the water was oppressive; he removed his cap and jerkin, and by so doing surprised the *hross* very much.

He rose cautiously to a standing position and surveyed the Malacandrian prospect which had opened on every side. Before and behind them lay the glittering lake, here studded with islands, and there smiling uninterruptedly at the pale blue sky; the sun, he noticed, was almost immediately overhead— they were in the Malacandrian tropics. At each end the lake vanished into more complicated groupings of land and water, softly, featherily embossed in the purple giant weed. But this marshy land or chain of archipelagoes, as he now beheld it, was bordered on each side with jagged walls of the pale green mountains, which he could still hardly call mountains, so tall they were, so gaunt, sharp, narrow and seemingly unbalanced. On the starboard they were not more than a mile away and seemed divided from the water only by a narrow strip of forest; to the left they were far more distant, though still impressive—perhaps seven miles from the boat. They ran on each side of the watered country as far as he could see, both onwards and behind them; he was sailing, in fact, on the flooded floor of a majestic canyon nearly ten miles wide and of unknown length. Behind and sometimes above the mountain peaks he could make out in many places great billowy piles of the rose-red substance which he had yesterday mistaken for cloud. The mountains, in fact, seemed to have no fall of ground behind them; they were rather the serrated bastion of immeasurable tablelands, higher in many places than themselves, which made the Malacandrian horizon left and right as far as eye could reach. Only straight ahead and straight astern was the planet cut with the vast gorge, which now appeared to him only as a rut or crack in the tableland.

He wondered what the cloud-like red masses were and endeavoured to ask by signs. The question was, however, too particular for sign-language. The *hross*, with a wealth of gesticulation—its arms or fore-limbs were more flexible than his and in quick motion almost whip-like—made it clear that it supposed him to be asking about the high ground in general. It named this *harandra*. The low, watered country, the gorge or canyon, appeared to be *handramit*. Ransom grasped the implications, *handra* earth, *harandra* high earth, mountain, *handramit*, low earth, valley. Highland and lowland, in fact. The peculiar importance of the distinction in Malacandrian geography he learned later.

By this time the *hross* had attained the end of its careful navigation. They were a couple of miles from land when it suddenly ceased paddling and sat tense with its paddle poised in the air; at the same moment the boat quivered and shot forward as if from a catapult. They had apparently availed themselves of some current. In a few seconds they were racing forward at some fifteen miles an hour and rising and falling on the strange, sharp, perpendicular waves of Malacandra with a jerky motion quite unlike that of the choppiest sea that Ransom had ever met on Earth. It reminded him of disastrous experiences on a trotting horse in the army; and it was intensely disagreeable. He gripped the gunwale with his left hand and mopped his brow with his right—the damp warmth from the water had become very troublesome. He wondered if the

Malacandrian food, and still more the Malacandrian drink, were really digestible by a human stomach. Thank heaven he was a good sailor! At least a fairly good sailor. At least——

Hastily he leaned over the side. Heat from blue water smote up to his face; in the depth he thought he saw eels playing: long, silver eels. The worst happened not once but many times. In his misery he remembered vividly the shame of being sick at a children's party . . . long ago in the star where he was born. He felt a similar shame now. It was not thus that the first representative of humanity would choose to appear before a new species. Did *hrossa* vomit too? Would it know what he was doing? Shaking and groaning, he turned back into the boat. The creature was keeping an eye on him, but its face seemed to him expressionless; it was only long after that he learned to read the Malacandrian face.

The current meanwhile seemed to be gathering speed. In a huge curve they swung across the lake to within a furlong of the farther shore, then back again, and once more onward, in giddy spirals and figures of eight, while purple wood and jagged mountain raced backwards and Ransom loathingly associated their sinuous course with the nauseous curling of the silver eels. He was rapidly losing all interest in Malacandra: the distinction between Earth and other planets seemed of no importance compared with the awful distinction of earth and water. He wondered despairingly whether the *hross* habitually lived on water. Perhaps they were going to spend the night in this detestable boat. . . .

His sufferings did not, in fact, last long. There came a blessed cessation of the choppy movement and a slackening of speed, and he saw that the *hross* was backing water rapidly. They were still afloat, with shores close on each side; between them a narrow channel in which the water hissed furiously— apparently a shallow. The *hross* jumped overboard, splashing abundance of warm water into the ship; Ransom, more cautiously and shakily, clambered after it. He was about up to his knees. To his astonishment, the *hross*, without any appearance of effort, lifted the boat bodily on to the top of its head, steadied it with one forepaw, and proceeded, erect as a Grecian caryatid, to the land. They walked forward—if the swing-

ing movement of the *hross's* short legs from its flexible hips
could be called walking—beside the channel. In a few minutes
Ransom saw a new landscape.

The channel was not only a shallow but a rapid—the first,
indeed, of a series of rapids by which the water descended
steeply for the next half-mile. The ground fell away before
them and the canyon—or *handramit*— continued at a very
much lower level. Its walls, however, did not sink with it, and
from his present position Ransom got a clearer notion of the
lie of the land. Far more of the highlands to left and right
were visible, sometimes covered with the cloud-like red swell-
ings, but more often level, pale and barren to where the
smooth line of their horizon marched with the sky. The mountain peaks now appeared only as the fringe or border of the
true highland, surrounding it as the lower teeth surround the
tongue. He was struck by the vivid contrast between *harandra*
and *handramit*. Like a rope of jewels the gorge spread beneath
him, purple, sapphire blue, yellow and pinkish white, a rich
and variegated inlay of wooded land and disappearing, reappearing, ubiquitous water. Malacandra was less like earth than
he had been beginning to suppose. The *handramit* was no true
valley rising and falling with the mountain chain it belonged
to. Indeed, it did not belong to a mountain chain. It was only
an enormous crack or ditch, of varying depth, running through
the high and level *harandra;* the latter, he now began to suspect, was the true 'surface' of the planet—certainly would appear as surface to a terrestrial astronomer. To the *handramit*
itself there seemed no end; uninterrupted and very nearly
straight, it ran before him, a narrowing line of colour, to
where it clove the horizon with a V-shaped indenture. There
must be a hundred miles of it in view, he thought; and he
reckoned that he had put some thirty or forty miles of it behind him since yesterday.

All this time they were descending beside the rapids to
where the water was level again and the *hross* could relaunch
its skiff. During this walk Ransom learned the words for boat,
rapid, water, sun and carry; the latter, as his first verb, interested him particularly. The *hross* was also at some pains to
impress upon him an association or relation which it tried to
convey by repeating the contrasted pairs of words *hrossa-han-
dramit* and *séroni-harandra*. Ransom understood him to mean

the *hrossa* lived down in the *handramit* and the *séroni* up on the *harandra*. What the deuce were *séroni*, he wondered. The open reaches of the *harandra* did not look as if anything lived up there. Perhaps the *hrossa* had a mythology—he took it for granted they were on a low cultural level—and the *séroni* were gods or demons.

The journey continued, with frequent, though decreasing, recurrences of nausea for Ransom. Hours later he realized that *séroni* might very well be the plural of *sorn*.

The sun declined, on their right. It dropped quicker than on Earth, or at least on those parts of Earth that Ransom knew, and in the cloudless sky it had little sunset pomp about it. In some other queer way which he could not specify it differed from the sun he knew; but even while he speculated the needle-like mountain-tops stood out black against it and the *handramit* grew dark, though eastward (to their left) the high country of the *harandra* still shone pale rose, remote and smooth and tranquil, like another and more spiritual world.

Soon he became aware that they were landing again, that they were treading solid ground, were making for the depth of the purple forest. The motion of the boat still worked in his fantasy and the earth seemed to sway beneath him; this, with weariness and twilight, made the rest of the journey dream-like. Light began to glare in his eyes. A fire was burning. It illuminated the huge leaves overhead, and he saw stars beyond them. Dozens of *hrossa* seemed to have surrounded him; more animal, less human, in their multitude and their close neighborhood to him, than his solitary guide had seemed. He felt some fear, but more a ghastly inappropriateness. He wanted men—any men, even Weston and Devine. He was too tired to do anything about these meaningless bullet heads and furry faces—could make no response at all. And then, lower down, closer to him, more mobile, came in throngs the whelps, the puppies, the cubs, whatever you called them. Suddenly his mood changed. They were jolly little things. He laid his hand on one black head and smiled; the creature scurried away.

He never could remember much of that evening. There was more eating and drinking, there was continual coming and going of black forms, there were strange eyes luminous in the firelight; finally, there was sleep in some dark, apparently covered place.

## Chapter 11

EVER SINCE he awoke on the space-ship Ransom had been thinking about the amazing adventure of going to another planet, and about his chances of returning from it. What he had not thought about was *being* on it. It was with a kind of stupefaction each morning that he found himself neither arriving in, nor escaping from, but simply living on, Malacandra; waking, sleeping, eating, swimming and even, as the days passed, talking. The wonder of it smote him most strongly when he found himself, about three weeks after his arrival, actually going for a walk. A few weeks later he had his favourite walks, and his favourite foods; he was beginning to develop habits. He knew a male from a female *hross* at sight, and even individual differences were becoming plain. Hyoi who had first found him—miles away to the north—was a very different person from the grey-muzzled, venerable Hnohra who was daily teaching him the language; and the young of the species were different again. They were delightful. You could forget all about the rationality of *hrossa* in dealing with them. Too young to trouble him with the baffling enigma of reason in an inhuman form, they solaced his loneliness, as if he had been allowed to bring a few dogs with him from the Earth. The cubs, on their part, felt the liveliest interest in the hairless goblin which had appeared among them. With them, and therefore indirectly with their dams, he was a brilliant success.

Of the community in general his earlier impressions were all gradually being corrected. His first diagnosis of their culture was what he called 'old stone age.' The few cutting instruments they possessed were made of stone. They seemed to have no pottery but a few clumsy vessels used for boiling, and boiling was the only cookery they attempted. Their common drink vessel, dish and ladle all in one, was the oyster-like shell in which he had first tasted *hross* hospitality; the fish which it contained was their only animal food. Vegetable fare they had in great plenty and variety, some of it delicious. Even the pinkish-white weed which covered the whole *handramit* was edible at a pinch, so that if he had starved before Hyoi found him he would have starved amidst abundance. No *hross*, however, ate the weed (*honodraskrud*) for choice, though it might be used *faute de mieux* on a journey. Their dwellings were beehive-shaped huts of stiff leaf and the villages—there were several in the neighbourhood—were always built beside rivers for warmth and well upstream towards the walls of the *handramit* where the water was hottest. They slept on the ground. They seemed to have no arts except a kind of poetry and music which was practised almost every evening by a team or troupe of four *hrossa*. One recited half chanting at great length while the other three, sometimes singly and sometimes antiphonally, interrupted him from time to time with song. Ransom could not find out whether these interruptions were simply lyrical interludes or dramatic dialogue arising out of the leader's narrative. He could make nothing of the music. The voices were not disagreeable and the scale seemed adapted to human ears, but the time-pattern was meaningless to his sense of rhythm. The occupations of the tribe or family were at first mysterious. People were always disappearing for a few days and reappearing again. There was a little fishing and much journeying in boats of which he never discovered the object. Then one day he saw a kind of caravan of *hrossa* setting out by land each with a load of vegetable food on its head. Apparently there was some kind of trade in Malacandra.

He discovered their agriculture in the first week. About a mile down the *handramit* one came to broad lands free of forest and clothed for many miles together in low pulpy vegetation in which yellow, orange and blue predominated. Later on, there were lettuce-like plants about the height of a terrestrial birch-tree. Where one of these overhung the warmth of water you could step into one of the lower leaves and lie deliciously as in a gently moving, fragrant hammock. Elsewhere it was not warm enough to sit still for long out of doors; the general temperature of the *handramit* was that of a fine winter's morning on Earth. These food-producing areas were worked communally by the surrounding villages, and division of labour had been carried to a higher point than he expected. Cutting, drying, storing, transport and something like manuring were all carried on, and he suspected that some at least of the water channels were artificial.

But the real revolution in his understanding of the *hrossa* began when he had learned enough of their language to attempt some satisfaction of their curiosity about himself. In answer to their questions he began by saying that he had come out of the sky. Hnohra immediately asked from which planet or earth (*handra*). Ransom, who had deliberately given a childish version of the truth in order to adapt it to the supposed ignorance of his audience, was a little annoyed to find Hnohra painfully explaining to him that he could not live in the sky because there was no air in it; he might have come through the sky but he must have come from a *handra*. He was quite unable to point Earth out to them in the night sky. They seemed surprised at his inability, and repeatedly pointed out to him a bright planet low on the western horizon—a little south of where the sun had gone down. He was surprised that they selected a planet instead of a mere star and stuck to their choice; could it be possible that they understood astronomy? Unfortunately he still knew too little of the language to explore their knowledge. He turned the conversation by asking them the name of the bright southern planet, and was told that it was Thulcandra—the silent world or planet.

'Why do you call it *Thulc?*' he asked. 'Why silent?' No one knew.

'The *séroni* know,' said Hnohra. 'That is the sort of thing they know.'

Then he was asked how he had come, and made a very poor attempt at describing the space-ship—but again:

'The *séroni* would know.'

Had he come alone? No, he had come with two others of his kind—bad men ('bent' men was the nearest *hrossian* equivalent) who tried to kill him, but he had run away from them. The *hrossa* found this very difficult, but all finally agreed that he ought to go to Oyarsa. Oyarsa would protect him. Ransom asked who Oyarsa was. Slowly, and with many misunderstandings, he hammered out the information that Oyarsa (1) lived at Meldilorn; (2) knew everything and ruled everyone; (3) had always been there; and (4) was not a *hross*, nor one of the *séroni*. Then Ransom, following his own idea, asked if Oyarsa had made the world. The *hrossa* almost barked in the fervour of their denial. Did people in Thulcandra not know that Maleldil the Young had made and still ruled the world? Even a child knew that. Where did Maleldil live, Ransom asked.

'With the Old One.'

And who was the Old One? Ransom did not understand the answer. He tried again.

'Where was the Old One?'

'He is not that sort,' said Hnohra, 'that he has to live anywhere,' and proceeded to a good deal which Ransom did not follow. But he followed enough to feel once more a certain irritation. Ever since he had discovered the rationality of the *hrossa* he had been haunted by a conscientious scruple as to whether it might not be his duty to undertake their religious instruction; now, as a result of his tentative efforts, he found himself being treated as if *he* were the savage and being given a first sketch of civilized religion—a sort of *hrossian* equivalent of the shorter catechism. It became plain that Maleldil was a spirit without body, parts or passions.

'He is not *hnau*,' said the *hrossa*.

'What is *hnau*?' asked Ransom.

'You are *hnau*. I am *hnau*. The *séroni* are *hnau*. The *pfifltriggi* are *hnau*.'

'*Pfifltriggi?*' said Ransom.

'More than ten days' journey to the west,' said Hnohra. 'The *harandra* sinks down not into a *handramit* but into a broad place, an open place, spreading every way. Five days' journey from the north to the south of it; ten days' journey from the east to the west. The forests are of other colours there than here, they are blue and green. It is very deep there, it goes to the roots of the world. The best things that can be dug out of the earth are there. The *pfifltriggi* live there. They delight in digging. What they dig they soften with fire and make things of it. They are little people, smaller than you, long in the snout, pale, busy. They have long limbs in front. No *hnau* can match them in making and shaping things as none can match us in singing. But let *Hmān* see.'

He turned and spoke to one of the younger *hrossa* and presently, passed from hand to hand, there came to him a little bowl. He held it close to the firelight and examined it. It was certainly of gold, and Ransom realized the meaning of Devine's interest in Malacandra.

'Is there much of this thing?' he asked.

Yes, he was told, it was washed down in most of the rivers; but the best and most was among the *pfifltriggi*, and it was they who were skilled in it. *Arbol hru*, they called it—Sun's blood. He looked at the bowl again. It was covered with fine etching. He saw pictures of *hrossa* and of smaller, almost frog-like animals; and then, of *sorns*. He pointed to the latter inquiringly.

'*Séroni*,' said the *hrossa*, confirming his suspicions. 'They live up almost on the *haranda*. In the big caves.'

The frog-like animals—or tapir-headed, frog-bodied animals—were *pfifltriggi*. Ransom turned it over in his mind. On Malacandra, apparently, three distinct species had reached rationality, and none of them had yet exterminated the other two. It concerned him intensely to find out which was the real master.

'Which of the *hnau* rule?' he asked.

'Oyarsa rules,' was the reply.

'Is he *hnau*?'

This puzzled them a little. The *séroni*, they thought, would be better at that kind of question. Perhaps Oyarsa was *hnau*, but a very different *hnau*. He had no death and no young.

'These *séroni* know more than the *hrossa*?' asked Ransom.

This produced more a debate than an answer. What emerged finally was the *séroni* or *sorns* were perfectly helpless in a boat, and could not fish to save their lives, could hardly swim, could make no poetry, and even when *hrossa* had made it for them could understand only the inferior sorts; but they were admittedly good at finding out things about the stars and understanding the darker utterances of Oyarsa and telling what happened in Malacandra long ago—longer ago than anyone could remember.

'Ah—the intelligentsia,' thought Ransom. 'They must be the real rulers, however it is disguised.'

He tried to ask what would happen if the *sorns* used their wisdom to make the *hrossa* do things—this was as far as he could get in his halting Malacandrian. The question did not sound nearly so urgent in this form as it would have done if he had been able to say 'used their scientific resources for the exploitation of their uncivilized neighbours.' But he might have spared his pains. The mention of the *sorns*' inadequate appreciation of poetry had diverted the whole conversation into literary channels. Of the heated, and apparently technical, discussion which followed he understood not a syllable.

Naturally his conversations with the *hrossa* did not all turn on Malacandra. He had to repay them with information about Earth. He was hampered in this both by the humiliating discoveries which he was constantly making of his own ignorance about his native planet, and partly by his determination to conceal some of the truth. He did not want to tell them too much of our human wars and industrialisms. He remembered how H. G. Wells's Cavor had met his end on the Moon; also he felt shy. A sensation akin to that of physical nakedness came over him whenever they questioned him too closely about men —the *hmāna* as they called them. Moreover, he was determined not to let them know that he had been brought there to be given to the *sorns;* for he was becoming daily more certain that these were the dominant species. What he did tell them fired the imagination of the *hrossa*: they all began making poems about the strange *handra* where the plants were hard like stone and the earth-weed green like rock and the waters cold and salt, and *hmāna* lived out on top, on the *harandra*.

They were even more interested in what he had to tell them of the aquatic animal with snapping jaws which he had fled from in their own world and even in their own *handramit*. It was a *hnakra*, they all agreed. They were intensely excited. There had not been a *hnakra* in the valley for many years. The youth of the *hrossa* got out their weapons—primitive harpoons with points of bone—and the very cubs began playing at *hnakra*-hunting in the shallows. Some of the mothers showed signs of anxiety and wanted the cubs to be kept out of the water, but in general the news of the *hnakra* seemed to be immensely popular. Hyoi set off at once to do something to his boat, and Ransom accompanied him. He wished to make himself useful, and was already beginning to have some vague capacity with the primitive *hrossian* tools. They walked together to Hyoi's creek, a stone's throw through the forest.

On the way, where the path was single and Ransom was following Hyoi, they passed a little she-*hross,* not much more
than a cub. She spoke as they passed, but not to them: her
eyes were on a spot about five yards away.

'Who do you speak to, Hrikki?' said Ransom.

'To the *eldil.*'

'Where?'

'Did you not see him?'

'I saw nothing.'

'There! There!' she cried suddenly. 'Ah! He is gone. Did
you not see him?'

'I saw no one.'

'Hyoi!' said the cub. 'the *hmān* cannot see the *eldil.*'

But Hyoi, continuing steadily on his way, was already out
of earshot, and had apparently noticed nothing. Ransom concluded that Hrikki was 'pretending' like the young of his own
species. In a few moments he rejoined his companion.

## Chapter 12

THEY WORKED HARD at Hyoi's boat till noon and then spread themselves on the weed close to the warmth of the creek, and began their midday meal. The war-like nature of their preparations suggested many questions to Ransom. He knew no word for war, but he managed to make Hyoi understand what he wanted to know. Did *séroni* and *hrossa* and *pfifltriggi* ever go out like this, with weapons, against each other?

'What for?' asked Hyoi.

It was difficult to explain. 'If both wanted one thing and neither would give it,' said Ransom, 'would the other at last come with force? Would they say, give it or we kill you?'

'What sort of thing?'

'Well—food, perhaps.'

'If the other *hnau* wanted food, why should we not give it to them? We often do.'

'But how if we had not enough for ourselves?'

'But Maleldil will not stop the plants growing.'

'Hyoi, if you had more and more young, would Maleldil broaden the *handramit* and make enough plants for them all?'

'The *séroni* know that sort of thing. But why should we have more young?'

Ransom found this difficult. At last he said:

'Is the begetting of young not a pleasure among the *hrossa?*'

'A very great one, *Hmān*. This is what we call love.'

'If a thing is a pleasure, a *hmān* wants it again. He might want the pleasure more often than the number of young that could be fed.'

It took Hyoi a long time to get the point.

'You mean,' he said slowly, 'that he might do it not only in one or two years of his life but again?'

'Yes.'

'But why? Would he want his dinner all day or want to sleep after he had slept? I do not understand.'

'But a dinner comes every day. This love, you say, comes only once while the *hross* lives?'

'But it takes his whole life. When he is young he has to look for his mate; and then he has to court her; then he begets young; then he rears them; then he remembers all this, and boils it inside him and makes it into poems and wisdom.'

'But the pleasure he must be content only to remember?'

'That is like saying "My food I must be content to eat." '

'I do not understand.'

'A pleasure is full grown only when it is remembered. You are speaking, *Hmān*, as if the pleasure were one thing and the memory another. It is all one thing. The *séroni* could say it better than I say it now. Not better than I could say it in a poem. What you call remembering is the last part of the pleasure, as the *crah* is the last part of a poem. When you and I met, the meeting was over very shortly, it was nothing. Now it is growing something as we remember it. But still we know very little about it. What it will be when I remember it as I lie down to die, what it makes in me all my days till then— that is the real meeting. The other is only the beginning of it. You say you have poets in your world. Do they not teach you this?'

'Perhaps some of them do,' said Ransom. 'But even in a poem does a *hross* never long to hear one splendid line over again?'

Hyoi's reply unfortunately turned on one of those points in their language which Ransom had not mastered. There were two verbs which both, as far as he could see, meant to *long* or *yearn;* but the *hrossa* drew a sharp distinction, even an opposition, between them. Hyoi seemed to him merely to be saying that every one would long for it (*wondelone*) but no one in his senses could long for it (*hluntheline*).

'And indeed,' he continued, 'the poem is a good example. For the most splendid line becomes fully splendid only by means of all the lines after it; if you went back to it you would find it less splendid than you thought. You would kill it. I mean in a good poem.'

'But in a bent poem, Hyoi?"

'A bent poem is not listened to, *Hmān.*'

'And how of love in a bent life?'

'How could the life of a *hnau* be bent?'

'Do you say, Hyoi, that there are no bent *hrossa*?'

Hyoi reflected. 'I have heard,' he said at last, 'of something like what you mean. It is said that sometimes here and there a cub of certain age gets strange twists in him. I have heard of one that wanted to eat earth; there might, perhaps, be somewhere a *hross* likewise that wanted to have the years of love prolonged. I have not heard of it, but it might be. I have heard of something stranger. There is a poem about a *hross* who lived long ago, in another *handramit,* who saw things all made two—two suns in the sky, two heads on a neck; and last of all they say that he fell into such a frenzy that he desired two mates. I do not ask you to believe it, but that is the story: that he loved two *hressni.*'

Ransom pondered this. Here, unless Hyoi was deceiving him, was a species naturally continent, naturally monogamous. And yet, was it so strange? Some animals, he knew, had regular breeding seasons; and if nature could perform the miracle of turning the sexual impulse outward at all, why could she not go further and fix it, not morally but instinctively, to a single object? He even remembered dimly having heard that some terrestrial animals, some of the 'lower' animals, were naturally monogamous. Among the *hrossa,* anyway, it was obvious that unlimited breeding and promiscuity were as rare as the rarest perversions. At last it dawned upon him that it was not they, but his own species, that were the puzzle. That the *hrossa* should have such instincts was mildly surprising; but how came it that the instincts of the *hrossa* so closely resembled the unattained ideals of that far-divided species Man whose instincts were so deplorably different? What was the history of Man? But Hyoi was speaking again.

'Undoubtedly,' he said. 'Maleldil made us so. How could there ever be enough to eat if everyone had twenty young? And how could we endure to live and let time pass if we were always crying for one day or one year to come back—if we did not know that every day in a life fills the whole life with expectation and memory and that these *are* that day?'

'All the same,' said Ransom, unconsciously nettled on behalf of his own world, 'Maleldil has let in the *hnakra.*'

'Oh, but that is so different. I long to kill this *hnakra* as he also longs to kill me. I hope that my ship will be the first and I first in my ship with my straight spear when the black jaws snap. And if he kills me, my people will mourn and my brothers will desire still more to kill him. But they will not wish that there were no *hnéraki;* nor do I. How can I make you understand, when you do not understand the poets? The *hnakra* is our enemy, but he is also our beloved. We feel in our hearts his joy as he looks down from the mountain of water in the north where he was born; we leap with him when he jumps the falls; and when winter comes, and the lake smokes higher than our heads, it is with his eyes that we see it and know that his roaming time is come. We hang images of him in our houses, and the sign of all the *hrossa* is a *hnakra.* In him the spirit of the valley lives; and our young play at being *hnéraki* as soon as they can splash in the shallows.'

'And then he kills them?'

'Not often them. The *hrossa* would be bent *hrossa* if they let him get so near. Long before he had come down so far we should have sought him out. No, *Hmān,* it is not a few deaths roving the world around him that make a *hnau* miserable. It is a bent *hnau* that would blacken the world. And I say also this. I do not think the forest would be so bright, nor the water so warm, nor love so sweet, if there were no danger in the lakes. I will tell you a day in my life that has shaped me; such a day as comes only once, like love, or serving Oyarsa in Meldilorn. Then I was young, not much more than a cub, when I went far, far up the *handramit* to the land where stars shine at midday and even water is cold. A great waterfall I climbed. I stood on the shore of Balki the pool, which is the place of most awe in all worlds. The walls of it go up for ever and ever and huge and holy images are cut in them, the work of old times. There is the fall called the Mountain of Water. Because I have stood there alone, Maleldil and I, for even Oyarsa sent me no word, my heart has been higher, my song deeper, all my days. But do you think it would have been so unless I had known that in Balki *hnéraki* dwelled? There I drank life because death was in the pool. That was the best of drinks save one.'

'What one?' asked Ransom.

'Death itself in the day I drink it and go to Maleldil.'

Shortly after that they rose and resumed their work. The

sun was declining as they came back through the wood. It occurred to Ransom to ask Hyoi a question.

'Hyoi,' he said, 'it comes into my head that when I first saw you, and before you saw me, you were already speaking. That was how I knew that you were *hnau*, for otherwise I should have thought you a beast, and run away. But who were you speaking to?'

'To an *eldil*.'

'What is that? I saw no one.'

'Are there no *eldila* in your world, *Hmān*? That must be strange.'

'But what are they?'

'They come from Oyarsa—they are, I suppose, a kind of *hnau*.'

'As we came out to-day I passed a child who said she was talking to an *eldil*, but I could see nothing.'

'One can see by looking at your eyes, *Hmān*, that they are different from ours. But *eldila* are hard to see. They are not like us. Light goes through them. You must be looking in the right place and the right time; and that is not likely to come about unless the *eldil* wishes to be seen. Sometimes you can mistake them for a sunbeam or even a moving of the leaves; but when you look again you see that it was an *eldil* and that it is gone. But whether your eyes can ever see them I do not know. The *séroni* would know that.'

# Chapter 13

THE WHOLE VILLAGE was astir next morning before the sunlight—already visible on the *harandra*—had penetrated the
forest. By the light of the cooking-fires Ransom saw an inces-
sant activity of *hrossa*. The females were pouring out steaming
food from clumsy pots; Hnohra was directing the transporta-
tion of piles of spears to the boats; Hyoi, in the midst of a
group of the most experienced hunters, was talking too rapidly
and too technically for Ransom to follow; parties were arriving from the neighbouring villages; and the cubs, squealing
with excitement, were running hither and thither among their
elders.

He found that his own share in the hunt had been taken for
granted. He was to be in Hyoi's boat, with Hyoi and Whin.
The two *hrossa* would take it in turns to paddle, while Ransom
and the disengaged *hross* would be in the bows. He understood the *hrossa* well enough now to know that they were making him the noblest offer in their power, and the Hyoi and
Whin were each tormented by the fear lest he should be
paddling when the *hnakra* appeared. A short time ago, in England, nothing would have seemed more impossible to Ransom
than to accept the post of honour and danger in an attack
upon an unknown but certainly deadly aquatic monster. Even
more recently, when he had first fled from the *sorns*, or when
he had lain pitying himself in the forest by night, it would
hardly have been in his power to do what he was intending to
do to-day. For his intention was clear. Whatever happened, he
must show that the human species also were *hnau*. He was
only too well aware that such resolutions might look very
different when the moment came, but he felt an unwonted
assurance that somehow or other he would be able to go
through with it. It was necessary, and the necessary was always possible. Perhaps, too, there was something in the air he
now breathed, or in the society of the *hrossa*, which had begun to work a change in him.

The lake was just giving back the first rays of the sun when

77

he found himself kneeling side by side with Whin, as he had been told to, in the bows of Hyoi's ship, with a little pile of throwing-spears between his knees and one in his right hand, stiffening his body against the motion as Hyoi paddled them out into their place. At least a hundred boats were taking part in the hunt. They were in three parties. The central, and far the smallest, was to work its way up the current by which Hyoi and Ransom had descended after their first meeting. Longer ships than he had yet seen, eight-paddled ships, were used for this. The habit of the *hnakra* was to float down the current whenever he could; meeting the ships, he would presumably dart out of it into the still water to left or right. Hence while the central party slowly beat up the current, the light ships, paddling far faster, would cruise at will up and down either side of it to receive the quarry as soon as he broke what might be called his 'cover.' In this game numbers and intelligence were on the side of the *hrossa;* the *hnakra* had speed on his side, and also invisibility, for he could swim under water. He was nearly invulnerable except through his open mouth. If the two hunters in the bows of the boat he made for muffed their shots, this was usually the last of them and of their boat.

In the light skirmishing parties there were two things a brave hunter could aim at. He could keep well back and close to the long-ships where the *hnakra* was most likely to break out, or he could get as far forward as possible in the hope of meeting the *hnakra* going at its full speed and yet untroubled by the hunt, and of inducing it, by a well-aimed spear, to leave the current then and there. One could thus anticipate the beaters and kill the beast—if that was how the matter ended— on one's own. This was the desire of Hyoi and Whin; and almost—so strongly they infected him—of Ransom. Hence, hardly had the heavy craft of the beaters begun their slow progress up-current amid a wall of foam when he found his own ship speeding northward as fast as Hyoi could drive her, already passing boat after boat and making for the freest water. The speed was exhilarating. In the cold morning the warmth of the blue expanse they were clearing was not unpleasant. Behind them arose, re-echoed from the remote rock pinnacles on either side of the valley, the bell-like, deep-mouthed voices of more than two hundred *hrossa*, more musical than a cry of hounds but closely akin to it in quality as in purport. Something long sleeping in the blood awoke in Ransom. It did not seem impossible at this moment that even he might be the *hnakra*-slayer; that the fame of *Hmān hnakra-punt* might be handed down to posterity in this world that knew no other man. But he had had such dreams before, and knew how they ended. Imposing humility on the newly risen riot of his feelings, he turned his eyes to the troubled water of the current which they were skirting, without entering, and watched intently.

For a long time nothing happened. He became conscious of the stiffness of his attitude and deliberately relaxed his muscles. Presently Whin reluctantly went aft to paddle, and Hyoi came forward to take his place. Almost as soon as the change had been effected, Hyoi spoke softly to him and said, without taking his eyes off the current:

There is an *eldil* coming to us over the water.'

Ransom could see nothing—or nothing that he could distinguish from imagination and the dance of sunlight on the lake. A moment later Hyoi spoke again, but not to him.

'What is it, sky-born?'

What happened next was the most uncanny experience Ransom had yet had on Malacandra. He heard the voice. It seemed to come out of the air, about a yard above his head, and it was almost an octave higher than the *hross's*—higher even than his own. He realized that a very little difference in his ear would have made the *eldil* as inaudible to him as it was invisible.

'It is the Man with you, Hyoi,' said the voice. 'He ought not to be there. He ought to be going to Oyarsa. Bent *hnau* of his own kind from Thulcandra are following him; he should go to Oyarsa. If they find him anywhere else there will be evil.'

'He hears you, sky-born,' said Hyoi. 'And have you no message for my wife? You know what she wishes to be told.'

'I have a message for Hleri,' said the *eldil*. 'But you will not be able to take it. I go to her now myself. All that is well. Only —let the Man go to Oyarsa.'

There was a moment's silence.

'He is gone,' said Whin. 'And we have lost our share in the hunt.'

'Yes,' said Hyoi with a sigh. 'We must put *Hmān* ashore and teach him the way to Meldilorn.'

Ransom was not so sure of his courage but that one part of him felt an instant relief at the idea of any diversion from their present business. But the other part of him urged him to hold on to his new-found manhood; now or never—with such companions or with none—he must leave a deed on his memory instead of one more broken dream. It was in obedience to something like conscience that he exclaimed:

'No, no. There is time for that after the hunt. We must kill the *hnakra* first.'

'Once an *eldil* has spoken,' began Hyoi, when suddenly Whin gave a great cry (a 'bark' Ransom would have called it three weeks ago) and pointed. There, not a furlong away, was the torpedo-like track of foam; and now, visible through a wall of foam, they caught the metallic glint of the monster's sides. Whin was paddling furiously. Hyoi threw and missed. As his first spear smote the water his second was already in the air. This time it must have touched the *hnakra*. He wheeled right out of the current. Ransom saw the great black pit of his mouth twice open and twice shut with its snap of shark-like teeth. He himself had thrown now—hurriedly, excitedly, with unpractised hand.

'Back,' shouted Hyoi to Whin who was already backing water with every pound of his vast strength. Then all became confused. He heard Whin shout 'Shore!' There came a shock that flung him forward almost into the *hnakra's* jaws and he found himself at the same moment up to his waist in water. It was at him the teeth were snapping. Then as he flung shaft after shaft into the great cavern of the gaping brute he saw Hyoi perched incredibly on its back—on its nose—bending forward and hurling from there. Almost at once the *hross* was dislodged and fell with a wide splash nearly ten yards away. But the *hnakra* was killed. It was wallowing on its side, bubbling out its black life. The water around him was dark and stank.

When he recollected himself they were all on shore, wet,

steaming, trembling with exertion and embracing one another. It did not now seem strange to him to be clasped to a breast of wet fur. The breath of the *hrossa* which, though sweet, was not human breath, did not offend him. He was one with them. That difficulty which they, accustomed to more than one rational species, had perhaps never felt, was now overcome. They were all *hnau*. They had stood shoulder to shoulder in the face of an enemy, and the shapes of their heads no longer mattered. And he, even Ransom, had come through it and not been disgraced. He had grown up.

They were on a little promontory free of forest, on which they had run aground in the confusion of the fight. The wreckage of the boat and the corpse of the monster lay confused together in the water beside them. No sound from the rest of the hunting party was audible; they had been almost a mile ahead when they met the *hnakra*. All three sat down to recover their breath.

'So,' said Hyoi, 'we are *hnakrapunti*. This is what I have wanted all my life.'

At that moment Ransom was deafened by a loud sound—a perfectly familiar sound which was the last thing he expected to hear. It was a terrestrial, human and civilized sound; it was even European. It was the crack of an English rifle; and Hyoi, at his feet, was struggling to rise and gasping. There was blood on the white weed where he struggled. Ransom dropped on his knees beside him. The huge body of the *hross* was too heavy for him to turn round. Whin helped him.

'Hyoi, can you hear me?' said Ransom with his face close to the round seal-like head. 'Hyoi, it is through me that this has happened. It is the other *hmāna* who have hit you, the bent two that brought me to Malacandra. They can throw death at a distance with a thing they have made. I should have told you. We are all a bent race. We have come here to bring evil on Malacandra. We are only half *hnau*—Hyoi . . .' His speech died away into the inarticulate. He did not know the words for 'forgive,' or 'shame,' or 'fault,' hardly the word for 'sorry.' He could only stare into Hyoi's distorted face in speechless guilt. But the *hross* seemed to understand. It was trying to say something, and Ransom laid his ear close to the working mouth. Hyoi's dulling eyes were fixed on his own, but the expression of a *hross* was not even now perfectly intelligible to him.

'*Hnā—hmā*,' it muttered and then, at last, *Hmān, hnakra-punt*.' Then there came a contortion of the whole body, a gush of blood and saliva from the mouth; his arms gave way under the sudden dead weight of the sagging head, and Hyoi's face became as alien and animal as it had seemed at their first meeting. The glazed eyes and the slowly stiffening, be-draggled fur were like those of any dead beast found in an earthly wood.

Ransom resisted an infantile impulse to break out into im-precations on Weston and Devine. Instead he raised his eyes to meet those of Whin who was crouching—*hrossa* do not kneel—on the other side of the corpse.

'I am in the hands of your people, Whin,' he said. 'They must do as they will. But if they are wise they will kill me and certainly they will kill the other two.'

'One does not kill *hnau*,' said Whin. 'Only Oyarsa does that. But these other, where are they?'

Ransom glanced around. It was open on the promontory but thick wood came down to where it joined the mainland, per-haps two hundred yards away.

'Somewhere in the wood,' he said. 'Lie down, Whin, here where the ground is lowest. They may throw from their thing again.'

He had some difficulty in making Whin do as he suggested. When both were lying in dead ground, their feet almost in the water, the *hross* spoke again.

'Why did they kill him?' he asked.

'They would not know he was *hnau*,' said Ransom. 'I have told you that there is only one kind of *hnau* in our world. They would think he was a beast. If they thought that, they would kill him for pleasure, or in fear, or' (he hesitated) 'be-cause they were hungry. But I must tell you the truth, Whin. They would kill even a *hnau*, knowing it to be *hnau*, if they thought its death would serve them.'

There was a short silence.

'I am wondering,' said Ransom, 'if they saw me. It is for

me they are looking. Perhaps if I went to them they would be content and come no farther into your land. But why do they not come out of the wood to see what they have killed?'

'Our people are coming,' said Whin, turning his head. Ransom looked back and saw the lake black with boats. The main body of the hunt would be with them in a few minutes.

'They are afraid of the *hrossa*,' said Ransom. 'That is why they do not come out of the wood. I will go to them, Whin.'

'No,' said Whin. 'I have been thinking. All this has come from not obeying the *eldil*. He said you were to go to Oyarsa. You ought to have been already on the road. You must go now.'

'But that will leave the bent *hmāna* here. They may do more harm.'

'They will not set on the *hrossa*. You have said they are afraid. It is more likely that we will come upon them. Never fear—they will not see us or hear us. We will take them to Oyarsa. But you must go now, as the *eldil* said.'

'Your people will think I have run away because I am afraid to look in their faces after Hyoi's death.'

'It is not a question of thinking but of what an *eldil* says. This is cubs' talk. Now listen, and I will teach you the way.'

The *hross* explained to him that five days' journey to the south the *handramit* joined another *handramit;* and three days' up this other *handramit* to west and north was Meldilorn and the seat of Oyarsa. But there was a shorter way, a mountain road, across the corner of the *harandra* between the two canyons, which would bring him down to Meldilorn on the second day. He must go into the wood before them and through it till he came to the mountain wall of the *handramit;* and he must work south along the roots of the mountains till he came to a road cut up between them. Up this he must go, and somewhere beyond the tops of the mountains he would come to the tower of Augray. Augray would help him. He could cut weed for his food before he left the forest and came into the rock country. Whin realized that Ransom might meet the other two *hmāna* as soon as he entered the wood.

'If they catch you,' he said 'then it will be as you say, they will come no farther into our land. But it is better to be taken on your way to Oyarsa than to stay here. And once you are on the way to him, I do not think he will let the bent ones stop you.'

Ransom was by no means convinced that this was the best plan either for himself or for the *hrossa*. But the stupor of humiliation in which he had lain ever since Hyoi fell forbade him to criticize. He was anxious only to do whatever they wanted him to do, to trouble them as little as was now possible, and above all to get away. It was impossible to find out how Whin felt; and Ransom sternly repressed an insistent, whining impulse to renewed protestations and regrets, self-accusations that might elicit some word of pardon. Hyoi with his last breath had called him *hnakra*-slayer; that was forgiveness generous enough and with that he must be content. As soon as he had mastered the details of his route he bade farewell to Whin and advanced alone towards the forest.

# Chapter 14

UNTIL HE reached the wood Ransom found it difficult to think of anything except the possibility of another rifle bullet from Weston or Devine. He thought that they probably still wanted him alive rather than dead, and this, combined with the knowledge that a *hross* was watching him, enabled him to proceed with at least external composure. Even when he had entered the forest he felt himself in considerable danger. The long branchless stems made 'cover' only if you were very far away from the enemy; and the enemy in this case might be very close. He became aware of a strong impulse to shout out to Weston and Devine and give himself up; it rationalized itself in the form that this would remove them from the district, as they would probably take him off to the *sorns* and leave the *hrossa* unmolested. But Ransom knew a little psychology and had heard of the hunted man's irrational instinct to give himself up—indeed, he had felt it himself in dreams. It was some such trick, he thought, that his nerves were now playing him. In any case he was determined henceforward to obey the *hrossa* or *eldila*. His efforts to rely on his own judgment in Malacandra had so far ended tragically enough. He made a strong resolution, defying in advance all changes of mood, that he would faithfully carry out the journey to Meldilorn if it could be done.

This resolution seemed to him all the more certainly right because he had the deepest misgivings about that journey. He understood that the *harandra*, which he had to cross, was the home of the *sorns*. In fact he was walking of his own free will into the very trap that he had been trying to avoid ever since his arrival on Malacandra. (Here the first change of mood tried to raise its head. He thrust it down.) And even if he got through the *sorns* and reached Meldilorn, who or what might Oyarsa be? Oyarsa, Whin had ominously observed, did not share the *hrossa's* objection to shedding the blood of a *hnau*. And again, Oyarsa ruled *sorns* as well as *hrossa* and *pfifltriggi*. Perhaps he was simply the arch-*sorn*. And now came the second change of mood. Those old terrestrial fears of some alien, cold intelligence, super-human in power, sub-human in cruelty, which had utterly faded from his mind among the *hrossa,* rose clamoring for readmission. But he strode on. He was going to Meldilorn. It was not possible, he told himself, that the *hrossa* should obey any evil or monstrous creature; and they had told him—or had they? he was not quite sure—that Oyarsa was not a *sorn.* Was Oyarsa a god?—perhaps that very idol to whom the *sorns* wanted to sacrifice him. But the *hrossa,* though they said strange things about him, clearly denied that he was a god. There was one God, according to them, Maleldil the Young; nor was it possible to imagine Hyoi or Hnohra worshipping a bloodstained idol. Unless, of course, the *hrossa* were after all under the thumb of the *sorns,* superior to their masters in all the qualities that human beings value, but intellectually inferior to them and dependent on them. It would be a strange but not an inconceivable world; heroism and poetry at the bottom, cold scientific intellect above it, and overtopping all some dark superstition which scientific intellect, helpless against the revenge of the emotional depths it had ignored, had neither will nor power to remove. A mumbo-jumbo . . . but Ransom pulled himself up. He knew too much now to talk that way. He and all his class would have called the *eldila* a superstition if they had been merely described to them, but now he had heard the voice himself. No, Oyarsa was a real person if he was a person at all.

He had now been walking for about an hour, and it was nearly midday. No difficulty about his direction had yet occurred; he had merely to keep going uphill and he was certain of coming out of the forest to the mountain wall sooner or later. Meanwhile he felt remarkably well, though greatly chastened in mind. The silent, purple half-light of the woods spread all around him as it had spread on the first day he spent in Malacandra, but everything else was changed. He looked back on that time as on a nightmare, on his own mood at that time as a sort of sickness. Then all had been whimpering, unanalysed, self-nourishing, self-consuming dismay. Now, in the clear light of an accepted duty, he felt fear indeed, but with it a sober sense of confidence in himself and in the world, and even an element of pleasure. It was the difference between a landsman in a sinking ship and a horseman on a bolting horse: either may be killed, but the horseman is an agent as well as a patient.

About an hour after noon he suddenly came out of the wood into bright sunshine. He was only twenty yards from the almost perpendicular bases of the mountain spires, too close to them to see their tops. A sort of valley ran up in the re-entrant between two of them at the the place where he had emerged: an unclimbable valley consisting of a single concave sweep of stone, which in its lower parts ascended steeply as the roof of a house and farther up seemed almost vertical. At the top it even looked as if it hung over a bit, like a tidal wave of stone at the very moment of breaking; but this, he thought, might be an illusion. He wondered what the *hrossa's* idea of a road might be.

He began to work his way southward along the narrow, broken ground between wood and mountain. Great spurs of the mountains had to be crossed every few moments, and even in that light-weight world it was intensely tiring. After about half an hour he came to a stream. Here he went a few paces into the forest, cut himself an ample supply of the ground-weed, and sat down beside the water's edge for lunch. When he had finished he filled his pockets with what he had not eaten and proceeded.

He began soon to be anxious about his road, for if he could make the top at all he could do it only by daylight, and the middle of the afternoon was approaching. But his fears were unnecessary. When it came it was unmistakable. An open way through the wood appeared on the left—he must be somewhere behind the *hross* village now—and on the right he saw the road, a single ledge or, in places, a trench, cut side-wise and upwards across the sweep of such a valley as he had seen before. It took his breath away—the insanely steep, hideously narrow staircase without steps, leading up and up from where he stood to where it was an almost invisible thread on the pale green surface of the rock. But there was no time to stand and look at it. He was a poor judge of heights, but he had no doubt that the top of the road was removed from him by a

more than Alpine distance. It would take him at least till sundown to reach it. Instantly he began the ascent.

Such a journey would have been impossible on earth; the
first quarter of an hour would have reduced a man of Ransom's build and age to exhaustion. Here he was at first delighted with the ease of his movement, and then staggered by
the gradient and length of the climb which, even under Malacandrian conditions, soon bowed his back and gave him an
aching chest and trembling knees. But this was not the worst.
He heard already a singing in his ears, and noticed that despite
his labour there was no sweat on his forehead. The cold, increasing at every step, seemed to sap his vitality worse than
any heat could have done. Already his lips were cracked; his
breath, as he panted, showed like a cloud; his fingers were
numb. He was cutting his way up into a silent arctic world,
and had already passed from an English to a Lapland winter.
It frightened him, and he decided that he must rest here or
not at all; a hundred paces more and if he sat down he would
sit for ever. He squatted on the road for a few minutes, slap-
ping his body with his arms. The landscape was terrifying. Already the *handramit* which had made his world for so many
weeks was only a thin purple cleft sunk amidst the boundless
level desolation of the *harandra* which now, on the farther
side, showed clearly between and above the mountain peaks.
But long before he was rested he knew that he must go on
or die.

The world grew stranger. Among the *hrossa* he had almost
lost the feeling of being on a strange planet; here it returned
upon him desolating force. It was no longer 'the world,'
scarcely even 'a world': it was a planet, a star, a waste place
in the universe, millions of miles from the world of men. It
was impossible to recall what he had felt about Hyoi, or Whin,
or the *eldila*, or Oyarsa. It seemed fantastic to have thought he
had duties to such hobgoblins—if they were not hallucinations
—met in the wilds of space. He had nothing to do with them:
he was a man. Why had Weston and Devine left him alone
like this?

But all the time the old resolution, taken when he could still
think, was driving him up the road. Often he forgot where he

was going, and why. The movement became a mechanical rhythm—from weariness to stillness, from stillness to unbearable cold, from cold to motion again. He noticed that the *handramit*—now an insignificant part of the landscape—was full of a sort of haze. He had never seen a fog while he was living there. Perhaps that was what the air of the *handramit* looked like from above; certainly it was different air from this. There was something more wrong with his lungs and heart than even the cold and the exertion accounted for. And though there was no snow, there was an extraordinary brightness. The light was increasing, sharpening and growing whiter; and the sky was a much darker blue than he had ever seen on Malacandra. Indeed, it was darker than blue; it was almost black, and the jagged spires of rock standing against it were like his mental picture of a lunar landscape. Some stars were visible.

Suddenly he realized the meaning of these phenomena. There was very little air above him: he was near the end of it. The Malacandrian atmosphere lay chiefly in the *handramits;* the real surface of the planet was naked or thinly clad. The stabbing sunlight and the black sky above him were that 'heaven' out of which he had dropped into the Malacandrian world, already showing through the last thin veil of air. If the top were more than a hundred feet away, it would be where no man could breathe at all. He wondered whether the *hrossa* had different lungs and had sent him by a road that meant death for man. But even while he thought of this he took note that those jagged peaks blazing in sunlight against an almost black sky were level with him. He was no longer ascending. The road ran on before him in a kind of shallow ravine bounded on his left by the tops of the highest rock pinnacles and on his right by a smooth ascending swell of stone that ran up to the true *harandra.* And where he was he could still breathe, though gasping, dizzy and in pain. The blaze in his eyes was worse. The sun was setting. The *hrossa* must have foreseen this; they could not live, any more than he, on the *harandra* by night. Still staggering forward, he looked about him for any sign of Augray's tower, whatever Augray might be.

Doubtless he exaggerated the time during which he thus wandered and watched the shadows from the rocks lengthening towards him. It cannot really have been long before he saw a light ahead—a light which showed how dark the surrounding landscape had become. He tried to run but his body would not respond. Stumbling in haste and weakness, he made for the light; thought he had reached it and found that it was far farther off than he had supposed; almost despaired; staggered on again, and came at last to what seemed a cavern mouth. The light within was an unsteady one and a delicious wave of warmth smote on his face. It was firelight. He came into the mouth of the cave and then, unsteadily, round the fire and into the interior, and stood still blinking in the light. When at last he could see, he discerned a smooth chamber of green rock, very lofty. There were two things in it. One of them, dancing on the wall and roof, was the huge, angular shadow of a *sorn;* the other, crouched beneath it, was the *sorn* himself.

## Chapter 15

'COME IN, Small One,' boomed the *sorn*. 'Come in and let me look at you.'

Now that he stood face to face with the spectre that had haunted him ever since he set foot on Malacandra, Ransom felt a surprising indifference. He had no idea what might be coming next, but he was determined to carry out his programme; and in the meantime the warmth and more breathable air were a heaven in themselves. He came in, well in past the fire, and answered the *sorn*. His own voice sounded to him a shrill treble.

'The *hrossa* have sent me to look for Oyarsa,' he said.

The *sorn* peered at him. 'You are not from this world,' it said suddenly.

'No,' replied Ransom, and sat down. He was too tired to explain.

'I think you are from Thulcandra, Small One,' said the *sorn*.

'Why?' said Ransom.

'You are small and thick and that is how the animals ought to be made in a heavier world. You cannot come from Glundandra, for it is so heavy that if any animals could live there they would be flat like plates—even you, Small One, would break if you stood up on that world. I do not think you are from Parelandra, for it must be very hot; if any came from there they would not live when they arrived here. So I conclude you are from Thulcandra.'

'The world I came from is called Earth by those who live there,' said Ransom. 'And it is much warmer than this. Before I came into your cave I was nearly dead with cold and thin air.'

The *sorn* made a sudden movement with one of its long forelimbs. Ransom stiffened (though he did not allow himself to retreat), for the creature might be going to grab him. In fact, its intentions were kindly. Stretching back into the cave, it took from the wall what looked like a cup. Then Ransom saw that it was attached to a length of flexible tube. The *sorn* put it into his hands.

'Smell on this,' it said. 'The *hrossa* also need it when they pass this way.'

Ransom inhaled and was instantly refreshed. His painful shortness of breath was eased and the tension of chest and temples was relaxed. The *sorn* and the lighted cavern, hitherto vague and dream-like to his eyes, took on a new reality.

'Oxygen?' he asked; but naturally the English word meant nothing to the *sorn*.

'Are you called Augray?' he asked.

'Yes,' said the *sorn*. 'What are you called?'

'The animal I am is called Man, and therefore the *hrossa* call me *Hmān*. But my own name is Ransom.'

'Man—Ren-soom,' said the *sorn*. He noticed that it spoke differently from the *hrossa*, without any suggestion of their persistent initial H.

It was sitting on its long, wedge-shaped buttocks with its feet drawn close up to it. A man in the same posture would have rested his chin on his knees, but the *sorn's* legs were too long for that. Its knees rose high above its shoulders on each side of its head—grotesquely suggestive of huge ears—and the head, down between them, rested its chin on the protruding breast. The creature seemed to have either a double chin or a beard; Ransom could not make out which in the firelight. It was mainly white or cream in colour and seemed to be clothed down to the ankles in some soft substance that reflected the light. On the long fragile shanks, where the creature was closest to him, he saw that this was some natural kind of coat. It was not like fur but more like feathers. In fact it was almost exactly like feathers. The whole animal, seen at close quarters, was less terrifying than he had expected, and even a little smaller. The face, it was true, took a good deal of getting used to—it was too long, too solemn and too colourless, and it was much more unpleasantly like a human face than any inhuman creature's face ought to be. Its eyes, like those of all very large creatures, seemed too small for it. But it was more grotesque than horrible. A new conception of the *sorns* began to arise in his mind: the ideas of 'giant' and 'ghost' receded behind those of 'goblin' and 'gawk.'

'Perhaps you are hungry, Small One,' it said.

Ransom was. The *sorn* rose with strange spidery movements and began going to and fro about the cave, attended by its thin goblin shadow. It brought him the usual vegetable foods of Malacandra, and strong drink, with the very welcome addition of a smooth brown substance which revealed itself to nose, eye and palate, in defiance of all probability, as cheese. Ransom asked what it was.

The *sorn* began to explain painfully how the female of some animals secreted a fluid for the nourishment of its young, and would have gone on to describe the whole process of milking and cheesemaking, if Ransom had not interrupted it.

'Yes, yes,' he said. 'We do the same on Earth. What is the beast you use?'

'It is a yellow beast with a long neck. It feeds on the forests that grow in the *handramit*. The young ones of our people who are not yet fit for much else drive the beasts down there in the mornings and follow them while they feed; then before night they drive them back and put them in the caves.'

For a moment Ransom found something reassuring in the thought that the *sorns* were shepherds. Then he remembered that the Cyclops in Homer plied the same trade.

'I think I have seen one of your people at this very work,' he said. 'But the *hrossa*—they let you tear up their forests?'

'Why should they not?'

'Do you rule the *hrossa*?'

'Oyarsa rules them.'

'And who rules you?'

'Oyarsa.'

'But you know more than the *hrossa*?'

'The *hrossa* know nothing except about poems and fish and making things grow out of the ground.'

'And Oyarsa—is he a *sorn*?'

'No, no, Small One. I have told you he rules all *nau*' (so he pronounced *hnau*), 'and everything in Malacandra.'

'I do not understand this Oyarsa,' said Ransom. 'Tell me more.'

'Oyarsa does not die,' said the *sorn*. 'And he does not breed. He is the one of his kind who was put into Malacandra to rule it when Malacandra was made. His body is not like ours, nor yours; it is hard to see and the light goes through it.'

'Like an *eldil?*'

'Yes, he is the greatest of *eldila* who ever come to a *handra*.'

'What are these *eldila?*'

'Do you tell me, Small One, that there are no *eldila* in your world?'

'Not that I know of. But what are *eldila,* and why can I not see them? Have they no bodies?'

'Of course they have bodies. There are a great many bodies you cannot see. Every animal's eyes see some things but not others. Do you know of many kinds of body in Thulcandra?'

Ransom tried to give the *sorn* some idea of the terrestrial terminology of solids, liquids and gases. It listened with great attention.

'That is not the way to say it,' it replied. 'Body is movement. If it is at one speed, you smell something; if at another, you hear a sound; if at another you see a sight; if at another, you neither see nor hear nor smell, nor know the body in any way. But mark this, Small One, that the two ends meet.'

'How do you mean?'

'If movement is faster, then that which moves is more nearly in two places at once.'

'That is true.'

'But if the movement were faster still—it is difficult, for you do not know many words—you see that if you made it faster and faster, in the end the moving thing would be in all places at once, Small One.'

'I think I see that.'

'Well, then, that is the thing at the top of all bodies—so fast that it is at rest, so truly body that it has ceased being body at all. But we will not talk of that. Start from where we are, Small One. The swiftest thing that touches our senses is light. We do not truly see light, we only see slower things lit by it, so that for us light is on the edge—the last thing we know before things become too swift for us. But the body of an *eldil* is a movement swift as light; you may say its body is made of light, but not of that which is light for the *eldil*. His "light" is a swifter movement which for us is nothing at all; and what we call light is for him a thing like water, a visible thing, a thing he can touch and bathe in—even a dark thing when not illumined by the swifter. And what we call firm things—flesh and earth—seem to him thinner, and harder to see, than our light, and more like clouds, and nearly nothing. To us the *eldil* is a thin, half-real body that can go through walls and rocks: to himself he goes through them because he is solid and firm and they are like cloud. And what is true light to him and fills the heaven, so that he will plunge into the rays of the sun to refresh himself from it, is to us the black nothing in the sky at night. These things are not strange, Small One, though they are beyond our senses. But it is strange that the *eldila* never visit Thulcandra.'

'Of that I am not certain,' said Ransom. It had dawned on him that the recurrent human tradition of bright, elusive people sometimes appearing on the Earth—*albs*, *devas* and the like—might after all have another explanation than the anthropologists had yet given. True, it would turn the universe rather oddly inside out; but his experiences in the space-ship had prepared him for some such operation.

'Why does Oyarsa send for me?' he asked.

'Oyarsa has not told me,' said the *sorn*. 'But doubtless he would want to see any stranger from another *handra*.'

'We have no Oyarsa in my world,' said Ransom.

'That is another proof,' said the *sorn*, 'that you come from Thulcandra, the silent planet.'

'What has that to do with it?'

The *sorn* seemed surprised. 'It is not very likely if you had an Oyarsa that he would never speak to ours.'

'Speak to yours? But how could he—it is millions of miles away.'

'Oyarsa would not think of it like that.'

'Do you mean that he ordinarily receives messages from other planets?'

'Once again, he would not say it that way. Oyarsa would not say that he lives on Malacandra and that another Oyarsa lives on another earth. For him Malacandra is only a place in the heavens; it is in the heavens that he and the others live. Of course they talk together. . . .'

Ransom's mind shied away from the problem; he was getting sleepy and thought he must be misunderstanding the *sorn*.

'I think I must sleep, Augray,' he said. 'And I do not know what you are saying. Perhaps, too, I do not come from what you call Thulcandra.'

'We will both sleep presently,' said the *sorn*. 'But first I will show you Thulcandra.'

It rose and Ransom followed it into the back of the cave. Here he found a little recess and running up within it a winding stair. The steps, hewn for *sorns*, were too high for a man to climb with any comfort, but using hands and knees he managed to hobble up. The *sorn* preceded him. Ransom did not understand the light, which seemed to come from some small round object which the creature held in its hand. They went up a long way, almost as if they were climbing up the inside of a hollow mountain. At last, breathless, he found himself in a dark but warm chamber of rock, and heard the *sorn* saying:

'She is still well above the southern horizon.' It directed his attention to something like a small window. Whatever it was, it did not appear to work like an earthly telescope, Ransom thought; though an attempt, made next day, to explain the principles of the telescope to the *sorn* threw grave doubts on his own ability to discern the difference. He leaned forward with his elbows on the sill of the aperture and looked. He saw perfect blackness and, floating in the centre of it, seemingly an arm's length away, a bright disk about the size of a half-crown. Most of its surface was featureless, shining silver; towards the bottom markings appeared, and below them a white cap, just as he had seen the polar caps in astronomical photographs of Mars. He wondered for a moment if it was Mars he was looking at; then, as his eyes took in the markings better, he recognized what they were—Northern Europe and a piece of North America. They were upside down with the North Pole at the bottom of the picture and this somehow shocked him. But it was Earth he was seeing—even, perhaps, England, though the picture shook a little and his eyes were quickly getting tired, and he could not be certain that he was not imagining it. It was all there in that little disk—London, Athens, Jerusalem, Shakespeare. There everyone had lived and everything had happened; and there, presumably, his pack was still lying in the porch of an empty house near Sterk.

'Yes,' he said dully to the *sorn*. 'That is my world.' It was the bleakest moment in all his travels.

# Chapter 16

RANSOM AWOKE next morning with the vague feeling that a great weight had been taken off his mind. Then he remembered that he was the guest of a *sorn* and that the creature he had been avoiding ever since he landed had turned out to be as amicable as the *hrossa*, though he was far from feeling the same affection for it. Nothing then remained to be afraid of in Malacandra except Oyarsa . . . 'The last fence,' thought Ransom.

Augray gave him food and drink.

'And now,' said Ransom, 'how shall I find my way to Oyarsa?'

'I will carry you,' said the *sorn*. 'You are too small a one to make the journey yourself and I will gladly go to Meldilorn. The *hrossa* should not have sent you this way. They do not seem to know from looking at an animal what sort of lungs it has and what it can do. It is just like a *hross*. If you died on the *harandra* they would have made a poem about the gallant *hmān* and how the sky grew black and the cold stars shone and he journeyed on and journeyed on; and they would have put in a fine speech for you to say as you were dying . . . and all this would seem to them just as good as if they had used a little forethought and saved your life by sending you the easier way round.'

'I like the *hrossa*,' said Ransom a little stiffly. 'And I think the way they talk about death is the right way.'

'They are right not to fear it, Ren-soom, but they do not seem to look at it reasonably as part of the very nature of our bodies—and therefore often avoidable at times · when they would never see how to avoid it. For example, this has saved the life of many a *hross*, but a *hross* would not have thought of it.'

He showed Ransom a flask with a tube attached to it, and at the end of the tube a cup, obviously an apparatus for administering oxygen to oneself.

'Smell on it as you have need, Small One,' said the *sorn*. 'And close it up when you do not.'

Augray fastened the thing on his back and gave the tube over his shoulder into his hand. Ransom could not restrain a shudder at the touch of the *sorn's* hands upon his body; they were fan-shaped, seven-fingered, mere skin over bone like a bird's leg, and quite cold. To divert his mind from such reactions he asked where the apparatus was made, for he had as yet seen nothing remotely like a factory or a laboratory.

'We thought it,' said the *sorn*, 'and the pfifltriggi made it.'

'Why do they make them?' said Ransom. He was trying once more, with his insufficient vocabulary, to find out the political and economic framework of Malacandrian life.

'They like making things,' said Augray. 'It is true they like best the making of things that are only good to look at and of no use. But sometimes when they are tired of that they will make things for us, things we have thought, provided they are difficult enough. They have not the patience to make easy things however useful they would be. But let us begin our journey. You shall sit on my shoulder.'

The proposal was unexpected and alarming, but seeing that the *sorn* had already crouched down, Ransom felt obliged to climb on to the plume-like surface of its shoulder, to seat himself beside the long, pale face, casting his right arm as far as it would go round the huge neck, and to compose himself as well as he could for this precarious mode of travel. The giant rose cautiously to a standing position and he found himself looking down on the landscape from a height of about eighteen feet.

'Is all well, Small One?' it asked.

'Very well,' Ransom answered, and the journey began.

Its gait was perhaps the least human thing about it. It lifted its feet very high and set them down very gently. Ransom was reminded alternately of a cat stalking, a strutting barndoor fowl, and a high-stepping carriage horse; but the movement was not really like that of any terrestrial animal. For the passenger it was surprisingly comfortable. In a few minutes he had lost all sense of what was dizzying or unnatural in his position. Instead, ludicrous and even tender associations came crowding into his mind. It was like riding an elephant at the zoo in boyhood—like riding on his father's back at a still earlier age. It was fun. They seemed to be doing between six and seven miles an hour. The cold, though severe, was endurable; and thanks to the oxygen he had little difficulty with his breathing.

The landscape which he saw from his high, swaying post of observation was a solemn one. The *handramit* was nowhere to be seen. On each side of the shallow gully in which they were walking, a world of naked, faintly greenish rock, interrupted with wide patches of red, extended to the horizon. The heaven, darkest blue where the rock met it, was almost black at the zenith, and looking in any direction where sunlight did not blind him, he could see the stars. He learned from the *sorn* that he was right in thinking they were near the limits of the breathable. Already on the mountain fringe that borders the *harandra* and walls the *handramit*, or in the narrow depression along which their road led them, the air is of Himalayan rarity, ill breathing for a *hross*, and a few hundred feet higher, on the *harandra* proper, the true surface of the planet, it admits no life. Hence the brightness through which they walked was almost that of heaven—celestial light hardly at all tempered with an atmospheric veil.

The shadow of the *sorn*, with Ransom's shadow on its shoulder, moved over the uneven rock unnaturally distinct like the shadow of a tree before the headlights of a car; and the rock beyond the shadow hurt his eyes. The remote horizon seemed but an arm's length away. The fissures and moulding of distant slopes were clear as the background of a primitive picture made before men learned perspective. He was on the very frontier of that heaven he had known in the spaceship, and rays that the air-enveloped worlds cannot taste were once more at work upon his body. He felt the old lift of the heart, the soaring solemnity, the sense, at once sober and ecstatic, of life and power offered in unasked and unmeasured abundance. If there had been air enough in his lungs he would have laughed aloud. And now, even in the immediate landscape, beauty was drawing near. Over the edge of the valley, as it had frothed down from the true *harandra*, came great curves of the rose-tinted, cumular stuff which he had seen so often from a distance. Now on a nearer view they appeared hard as stone in substance, but puffed above and stalked beneath like vegetation. His original simile of giant cauliflower turned out to be surprisingly correct—stone cauliflowers the size of cathedrals and the colour of pale rose. He asked the *sorn* what it was.

'It is the old forests of Malacandra,' said Augray. 'Once there was air on the *harandra* and it was warm. To this day, if you could get up there and live, you would see it all covered with the bones of ancient creatures; it was once full of life and noise. It was then these forests grew, and in and out among their stalks went a people that have vanished from the world these many thousand years. They were covered not with fur but with a coat like mine. They did not go in the water swimming or on the ground walking; they glided in the air on broad flat limbs which kept them up. It is said they were great singers, and in those days the red forests echoed with their music. Now the forests have become stone and only *eldila* can go among them.'

'We still have such creatures in our world,' said Ransom. 'We call them birds. Where was Oyarsa when all this happened to the *harandra*?'

'Where he is now.'

'And he could not prevent it?'

'I do not know. But a world is not made to last for ever, much less a race; that is not Maleldil's way.'

As they proceeded the petrified forests grew more numerous, and often for half an hour at a time the whole horizon of the lifeless, almost airless, waste blushed like an English garden in summer. They passed many caves where, as Augray told him, *sorns* lived; sometimes a high cliff would be perforated with countless holes to the very top and unidentifiable noises came hollowly from within. 'Work' was in progress, said the *sorn*, but of what kind it could not make him understand. Its vocabulary was very different from that of the *hrossa*. Nowhere did he see anything like a village or city of *sorns*, who were apparently solitary not social creatures. Once or twice a long pallid face would show from a cavern mouth and exchange a horn-like greeting with the travellers, but for the most part the long valley, the rock-street of the silent people, was still and empty as the *harandra* itself.

Only towards afternoon, as they were about to descend into a dip of the road, they met three *sorns* together coming towards them down the opposite slope. They seemed to Ransom to be rather skating than walking. The lightness of their world and the perfect poise of their bodies allowed them to lean forward at right angles to the slope, and they came swiftly down like full-rigged ships before a fair wind. The grace of their movement, their lofty stature, and the softened glancing of the sunlight on their feathery sides, effected a final transformation in Ransom's feelings towards their race. 'Ogres' he had called them when they first met his eyes as he struggled in the grip of Weston and Devine; 'Titans' or 'Angels' he now thought would have been a better word. Even the faces, it seemed to him, he had not then seen aright. He had thought them spectral when they were only august, and his human reaction to their lengthened severity of line and profound stillness of expression now appeared to him not so much cowardly as vulgar. So might Parmenides or Confucius look to the eyes of a Cockney schoolboy! The great white creatures sailed towards Ransom and Augray and dipped like trees and passed.

In spite of the cold—which made him often dismount and take a spell on foot—he did not wish for the end of the journey; but Augray had his own plans and halted for the night long before sundown at the home of an older *sorn*. Ransom saw well enough that he was brought there to be shown to a great scientist. The cave, or, to speak more correctly, the system of excavations, was large and many-chambered, and contained a multitude of things that he did not understand. He was specially interested in a collection of rolls, seemingly of skin, covered with characters, which were clearly books; but he gathered that books were few in Malacandra.

'It is better to remember,' said the *sorns*.

When Ransom asked if valuable secrets might not thus be lost, they replied that Oyarsa always remembered them and would bring them to light if he thought fit.

'The *hrossa* used to have many books of poetry,' they added. 'But now they have fewer. They say that the writing of books destroys poetry.'

Their host in these caverns was attended by a number of other *sorns* who seemed to be in some way subordinate to him; Ransom thought at first that they were servants but decided later that they were pupils or assistants.

The evening's conversation was not such as would interest a terrestrial reader, for the *sorns* had determined that Ransom should not ask, but answer, questions. Their questioning was very different from the rambling inquiries of the *hrossa*. They worked systematically from the geology of Earth to its present geography, and thence in turn to flora, fauna, human history, languages, politics and arts. When they found that Ransom could tell them no more on a given subject—and this happened pretty soon in most of their inquiries—they dropped it at once and went on to the next. Often they drew out of him indirectly much more knowledge than he consciously possessed, apparently working from a wide background of general science. A casual remark about trees when Ransom was trying to explain the manufacture of paper would fill up for them a gap in his sketchy answers to their botanical questions; his account of terrestrial navigation might illuminate mineralogy; and his description of the steam-engine gave them a better knowledge of terrestrial air and water than Ransom had ever had. He had decided from the outset that he would be quite frank, for he now felt that it would be not *hnau,* and also that it would be unavailing, to do otherwise. They were astonished at what he had to tell them of human history —of war, slavery and prostitution.

'It is because they have no Oyarsa,' said one of the pupils.

'It is because every one of them wants to be a little Oyarsa himself,' said Augray.

'They cannot help it,' said the old *sorn.* 'There must be rule, yet how can creatures rule themselves? Beasts must be ruled by *hnau* and *hnau* by *eldila* and *eldila* by Maleldil. These creatures have no *eldila.* They are like one trying to lift himself by his own hair—or one trying to see over a whole country when he is on a level with it—like a female trying to beget young on herself.'

Two things about our world particularly stuck in their minds. One was the extraordinary degree to which problems of lifting and carrying things absorbed our energy. The other was the fact that we had only one kind of *hnau*: they thought this must have far-reaching effects in the narrowing of sympathies and even of thought.

'Your thought must be at the mercy of your blood,' said the old *sorn*. 'For you cannot compare it with thought that floats on a different blood.'

It was a tiring and very disagreeable conversation for Ransom. But when at last he lay down to sleep it was not of the human nakedness nor of his own ignorance that he was thinking. He thought only of the old forests of Malacandra and of what it might mean to grow up seeing always so few miles away a land of colour that could never be reached and had once been inhabited.

## Chapter 17

EARLY NEXT DAY Ransom again took his seat on Augray's shoulder. For more than an hour they travelled through the same bright wilderness. Far to the north the sky was luminous with a cloud-like mass of dull red or ochre; it was very large and drove furiously westward about ten miles above the waste. Ransom, who had yet seen no cloud in the Malacandrian sky, asked what it was. The *sorn* told him it was sand caught up from the great northern deserts by the winds of that terrible country. It was often thus carried, sometimes at a height of seventeen miles, to fall again, perhaps in a *handramit*, as a choking and blinding dust-storm. The sight of it moving with menace in the naked sky served to remind Ransom that they were indeed on the *outside* of Malacandra—no longer dwelling in a world but crawling the surface of a strange planet. At last the cloud seemed to drop and burst far on the western horizon, where a glow, not unlike that of a conflagration, remained visible until a turn of the valley hid all that region from his view.

The same turn opened a new prospect to his eyes. What lay before him looked at first strangely like an earthly landscape —a landscape of grey downland ridges rising and falling like waves of the sea. Far beyond, cliffs and spires of the familiar green rock rose against the dark blue sky. A moment later he saw that what he had taken for downlands was but the ridged and furrowed surface of a blue-grey valley mist—a mist which would not appear a mist at all when they descended into the *handramit*. And already, as their road began descending, it was less visible and the many-coloured pattern of the low country showed vaguely through it. The descent grew quickly steeper; like the jagged teeth of a giant —a giant with very bad teeth—the topmost peaks of the mountain wall down which they must pass loomed up over the edge of their gully. The look of the sky and the quality of the light were infinitesimally changed. A moment later they stood on the edge of such a slope as by earthly standards would rather be called a precipice; down and down this face, to where it vanished in a purple blush of vegetation, ran their road. Ransom refused absolutely to make the descent on Augray's shoulder. The *sorn*, though it did not fully understand his objection, stooped for him to dismount, and proceeded, with that same skating and forward-sloping motion, to go down before him. Ransom followed, using gladly but stiffly his numb legs.

The beauty of this new *handramit* as it opened before him took his breath away. It was wider than that in which he had hitherto lived and right below him lay an almost circular lake —a sapphire twelve miles in diameter set in a border of purple forest. Amidst the lake there rose like a low and gently sloping pyramid, or like a woman's breast, an island of pale red, smooth to the summit, and on the summit a grove of such trees as man had never seen. Their smooth columns had the gentle swell of the noblest beech-trees: but these were taller than a cathedral spire on earth, and at their tops, they broke rather into flower than foliage; into golden flower bright as tulip, still as rock, and huge as summer cloud. Flowers indeed they were, not trees, and far down among their roots he caught a pale hint of slab-like architecture. He knew before his guide told him that this was Meldilorn. He did not know what he had expected. The old dreams which he had brought from Earth of some more than American complexity of offices or some engineers' paradise of vast machines had indeed been long laid aside. But he had not looked for anything quite so classic, so virginal, as this bright grove—lying so still, so secret, in its coloured valley, soaring with inimitable grace so many hundred feet into the wintry sunlight. At every step of his descent the comparative warmth of the valley came up to him more deliciously. He looked above—the sky was turning to a paler blue. He looked below—and sweet and faint the thin fragrance of the giant blooms came up to him. Distant crags were growing less sharp in outline, and surfaces less bright. Depth, dimness, softness and perspective were returning to the landscape. The lip or edge of rock from which they had started their descent was already far overhead; it seemed unlikely that they had really come from there. He was breathing freely. His toes, so long benumbed, could move delightfully inside his boots. He lifted the ear-flaps of his cap and found his ears instantly filled with the sound of falling water. And now he was treading on soft ground-weed over level earth and the forest roof was above his head. They had conquered the *harandra* and were on the threshold of Meldilorn.

A short walk brought them into a kind of forest 'ride'—a broad avenue running straight as an arrow through the purple stems to where the vivid blue of the lake danced at the end of it. There they found a gong and hammer hung on a pillar of stone. These objects were all richly decorated, and the gong and hammer were of a greenish blue metal which Ransom did not recognize. Augray struck the gong. An excitement was rising in Ransom's mind which almost prevented him from examining as coolly as he wished the ornamentation of the stone. It was partly pictorial, partly pure decoration. What chiefly struck him was a certain balance of packed and empty surfaces. Pure line drawings, as bare as the prehistoric pictures of reindeer on Earth, alternated with patches of design as close and intricate as Norse or Celtic jewellery; and then, as you looked at it, these empty and crowded areas turned out to be themselves arranged in larger designs. He was struck by the fact that the pictorial work was not confined to the emptier spaces; quite often large arabesques included as a subordinate detail intricate pictures. Elsewhere the opposite plan had been followed—and this alternation, too, had a rhythmical or patterned element in it. He was just beginning to find out that the pictures, though stylized, were obviously intended to tell a story, when Augray interrupted him. A ship had put out from the island shore of Meldilorn.

As it came towards them Ransom's heart warmed to see that was paddled by a *hross*. The creature brought its boat up to the shore where they were waiting, stared at Ransom and then looked inquiringly at Augray.

'You may well wonder at this *hnau*, Hrinha,' said the *sorn*, 'for you have never seen anything like it. It is called Ren-soom and has come through heaven from Thulcandra.'

'It is welcome, Augray,' said the *hross* politely. 'Is it coming to Oyarsa?'

'He has sent for it.'

'And for you also, Augray?'

'Oyarsa has not called me. If you will take Ren-soom over the water, I will go back to my tower.'

The *hross* indicated that Ransom should enter the boat. He attempted to express his thanks to the *sorn* and after a moment's consideration unstrapped his wrist-watch and offered it to him; it was the only thing he had which seemed a suitable present for a *sorn*. He had no difficulty in making Augray understand its purpose; but after examining it the giant gave it back to him, a little reluctantly, and said:

'This gift ought to be given to a *pfifltrigg*. It rejoices my heart, but they would make more of it. You are likely to meet some of the busy people in Meldilorn: give it to them. As for its use, do your people not know except by looking at this thing how much of the day has worn?'

'I believe there are beasts that have a sort of knowledge of that,' said Ransom, 'but our *hnau* have lost it.'

After this, his farewells to the *sorn* were made and he embarked. To be once more in a boat and with a *hross*, to feel the warmth of water on his face and to see a blue sky above him, was almost like coming home. He took off his cap and leaned back luxuriously in the bows, plying his escort with questions. He learned that the *hrossa* were not specially concerned with the service of Oyarsa, as he had surmised from finding a *hross* in charge of the ferry: all three species of *hnau* served him in their various capacities, and the ferry was naturally entrusted to those who understood boats. He learned that his own procedure on arriving in Meldilorn must be to go where he liked and do what he pleased until Oyarsa called for him. It might be an hour or several days before this happened. He would find huts near the landing-place where he could sleep if necessary and where food would be given him. In return he related as much as he could make intelligible of his own world and his journey from it; and he warned the *hross* of the dangerous bent men who had brought him and who were still at large on Malacandra. As he did so, it occurred to him that he had not made this sufficiently clear to Augray; but he consoled himself with the reflection that Weston and Devine seemed to have already some liaison with the *sorns* and that they would not be likely to molest things so large and so comparatively man-like. At any rate, not yet. About De-vine's ultimate designs he had no illusions; all he could do was to make a clean breast of them to Oyarsa. And now the ship touched land.

Ranson rose, while the *hross* was making fast, and looked about him. Close to the little harbour which they had entered, and to the left, were low buildings of stone—the first he had seen in Malacandra—and fires were burning. There, the *hross* told him, he could find food and shelter. For the rest the island seemed desolate, and its smooth slopes empty up to the grove that crowned them, where, again, he saw stonework. But this appeared to be neither temple nor house in the human sense, but a broad avenue of monoliths—a much larger Stonehenge, stately, empty and vanishing over the crest of the hill into the pale shadow of the flower-trunks. All was solitude; but as he gazed upon it he seemed to hear, against the background of morning silence, a faint, continual agitation of silvery sound—hardly a sound at all, if you attended to it, and yet impossible to ignore.

'The island is all full of *eldila*,' said the *hross* in a hushed voice.

He went ashore. As though half expecting some obstacle, he took a few hesitant paces forward and stopped, and then went on again in the same fashion.

Though the ground-weed was unusually soft and rich and his feet made no noise upon it, he felt an impulse to walk on tiptoes. All his movements became gentle and sedate. The width of water about this island made the air warmer than any he had yet breathed in Malacandra; the climate was almost that of a warm earthly day in late September—a day that is warm but with a hint of frost to come. The sense of awe which was increasing upon him deterred him from ap-proaching the crown of the hill, the grove and the avenue of standing stones.

He ceased ascending about half-way up the hill and began walking to his right, keeping a constant distance from the shore. He said to himself that he was having a look at the island, but his feeling was rather that the island was having a look at him. This was greatly increased by a discovery he made after he had been walking for about an hour, and which he ever afterwards found great difficulty in describing. In the most abstract terms it might be summed up by saying that the surface of the island was subject to tiny variations of light and shade which no change in the sky accounted for. If the air had not been calm and the ground-weed too short and firm to move in the wind, he would have said that a faint breeze was playing with it, and working such slight alterations in the shading as it does in a corn-field on the Earth. Like the silvery noises in the air, these footsteps of light were shy of observation. Where he looked hardest they were least to be seen: on the edges of his field of vision they came crowding as though a complex arrangement of them were there in progress. To attend to any one of them was to make it invisible, and the minute brightness seemed often to have just left the spot where his eyes fell. He had no doubt that he was 'seeing'—as much as he ever would see—the *eldila*. The sensation it produced in him was curious. It was not exactly uncanny, not as if he were surrounded by ghosts. It was not even as if he were being spied upon; he had rather the sense of being looked at by things that had a right to look. His feeling was less than fear; it had in it something of embarrassment, something of shyness, something of submission, and it was profoundly uneasy.

He felt tired and thought that in this favoured land it would be warm enough to rest out of doors. He sat down. The softness of the weed, the warmth and the sweet smell which pervaded the whole island, reminded him of Earth and gardens in summer. He closed his eyes for a moment; then he opened them again and noticed buildings below him, and over the lake he saw a boat approaching. Recognition suddenly came to him. That was the ferry, and these buildings were the guest-house beside the harbour; he had walked all round the island. A certain disappointment succeeded this discovery. He was beginning to feel hungry. Perhaps it would be a good plan to go down and ask for some food; at any rate it would pass the time.

But he did not do so. When he rose and looked more closely at the guest-house he saw a considerable stir of creatures about it, and while he watched he saw that a full load of passengers was landing from the ferry-boat. In the lake he saw some moving objects which he did not at first identify but which turned out to be *sorns* up to their middles in the water and obviously wading to Meldilorn from the mainland. There were about ten of them. For some reason or other the island was receiving an influx of visitors. He no longer supposed that any harm would be done to him if he went down and mixed in the crowd, but he felt a reluctance to do so. The situation brought vividly back to his mind his experience as a new boy at school—new boys came a day early—hanging about and watching the arrival of the old hands. In the end he decided not to go down. He cut and ate some of the ground-weed and dozed for a little.

In the afternoon, when it grew colder, he resumed his walking. Other *hnau* were roaming about the island by this time. He saw *sorns* chiefly, but this was because their height made them conspicuous. There was hardly any noise. His reluctance to meet these fellow-wanderers, who seemed to confine themselves to the coast of the island, drove him half consciously upwards and inwards. He found himself at last on the fringes of the grove and looking straight up the monolithic avenue. He had intended, for no very clearly defined reason, not to enter it, but he fell to studying the stone nearest to him, which was richly sculptured on all its four sides, and after that curiosity led him on from stone to stone.

The pictures were very puzzling. Side by side with representations of *sorns* and *hrossa* and what he supposed to be *pfifltriggi* there occurred again and again an upright wavy figure with only the suggestion of a face, and with wings. The wings were perfectly recognizable, and this puzzled him very much. Could it be that the traditions of Malacandrian art went back to that earlier geological and biological era when, as Augray had told him, there was life, including bird-life, on the *harandra*? The answer of the stones seemed to be Yes. He saw pictures of the old red forests with unmistakable birds flying among them, and many other creatures that he did not know. On another stone many of these were represented lying dead, and a fantastic *hnakra*-like figure, presumably symbolizing the cold, was depicted in the sky above them shooting at them with darts. Creatures still alive were crowding round the winged, wavy figure, which he took to be Oyarsa, pictured as

a winged flame. On the next stone Oyarsa appeared, followed
by many creatures, and apparently making a furrow with some
pointed instrument. Another picture showed the furrow being
enlarged by *pfifltriggi* with digging tools. *Sorns* were piling the
earth up in pinnacles on each side, and *hrossa* seemed to be
making water channels. Ransom wondered whether this were
a mythical account of the making of *handramits* or whether
they were conceivably artificial in fact.

Many of the pictures he could make nothing of. One that
particularly puzzled him showed at the bottom a segment of
a circle, behind and above which rose three-quarters of a disk
divided into concentric rings. He thought it was a picture of
the sun rising behind a hill; certainly the segment at the
bottom was full of Malacandrian scenes—Oyarsa in Meldilorn,
*sorns* on the mountain edge of the *harandra,* and many other
things both familiar to him and strange. He turned from it
to examine the disk which rose behind it. It was not the sun.
The sun was there, unmistakably, at the centre of the disk:
round this the concentric circles revolved. In the first and
smallest of these was pictured a little ball, on which rode a
winged figure something like Oyarsa, but holding what appeared to be a trumpet. In the next, a similar ball carried
another of the flaming figures. This one, instead of even the
suggested face, had two bulges which after long inspection
he decided were meant to be the udders or breasts of a female
mammal. By this time he was quite sure that he was looking
at a picture of the solar-system. The first ball was Mercury,
the second Venus—'And what an extraordinary coincidence,'
thought Ransom, 'that their mythology, like ours, associates
some idea of the female with Venus.' The problem would have
occupied him longer if a natural curiosity had not drawn his
eyes on to the next ball which must represent the Earth. When
he saw it, his whole mind stood still for a moment. The ball
was there, but where the flame-like figure should have been,
a deep depression of irregular shape had been cut as if to erase
it. Once, then—but his speculations faltered and became silent
before a series of unknowns. He looked at the next circle.
Here there was no ball. Instead, the bottom of this circle
touched the top of the big segment filled with Malacandrian
scenes, so that Malacandra at this point touched the solar

system and came out of it in perspective towards the spectator. Now that his mind had grasped the design, he was astonished at the vividness of it all. He stood back and drew a deep breath preparatory to tackling some of the mysteries in which he was engulfed. Malacandra, then, was Mars. The Earth—but at this point a sound of tapping or hammering, which had been going on for some time without gaining admission to his consciousness, became too insistent to be ignored. Some creature, and certainly not an *eldil*, was at work, close to him. A little startled—for he had been deep in thought—he turned round. There was nothing to be seen. He shouted out, idiotically, in English:

'Who's there?'

The tapping instantly stopped and a remarkable face appeared from behind a neighbouring monolith.

It was hairless like a man's or a *sorn's*. It was long and pointed like a shrew's, yellow and shabby-looking, and so low in the forehead that but for the heavy development of the head at the back and behind the ears (like a bag-wig) it could not have been that of an intelligent creature. A moment later the whole of the thing came into view with a startling jump. Ransom guessed that it was a *pfifltrigg*—and was glad that he had not met one of this third race on his first arrival in Malacandra. It was much more insect-like or reptilian than anything he had yet seen. Its build was distinctly that of a frog, and at first Ransom thought it was resting, frog-like, on its 'hands.' Then he noticed that that part of its fore-limbs on which it was supported was really, in human terms, rather an elbow than a hand. It was broad and padded and clearly made to be walked on; but upwards from it, at an angle of about forty-five degrees, went the true fore-arms—thin, strong fore-arms, ending in enormous, sensitive, many-fingered hands. He realized that for all manual work from mining to cutting cameos this creature had the advantage of being able to work with its full strength from a supported elbow. The insect-like effect was due to the speed and jerkiness of its movements and to the fact that it could swivel its head almost all the way round like a mantis; and it was increased by a kind of dry, rasping, jingling quality in the noise of its moving. It was rather like a grasshopper, rather like one of Arthur Rackham's dwarfs, rather like a frog, and rather like a little, old taxidermist whom Ransom knew in London.

'I come from another world,' began Ransom.

'I know, I know,' said the creature in a quick, twittering, rather impatient voice. 'Come here, behind the stone. This way, this way. Oyarsa's orders. Very busy. Must begin at once. Stand there.'

Ransom found himself on the other side of the monolith, staring at a picture which was still in process of completion. The ground was liberally strewn with chips and the air was full of dust.

'There,' said the creature. 'Stand still. Don't look at me. Look over there.'

For a moment Ransom did not quite understand what was expected of him; then, as he saw the *pfifltrigg* glancing to and fro at him and at the stone with the unmistakable glance of artist from model to work which is the same in all worlds, he realized and almost laughed. He was standing for his portrait! From his position he could see that the creature was cutting the stone as if it were cheese and the swiftness of its movements almost baffled his eyes, but he could get no impression of the work done, though he could study the *pfifltrigg*. He saw that the jingling and metallic noise was due to the number of small instruments which it carried about its body. Sometimes, with an exclamation of annoyance, it would throw down the tool it was working with and select one of these; but the majority of those in immediate use it kept in its mouth. He realized also that this was an animal artificially clothed like himself, in some bright scaly substance which appeared richly decorated though coated in dust. It had folds of furry clothing about its throat like a comforter, and its eyes were protected by dark bulging goggles. Rings and chains of a bright metal—not gold, he thought—adorned its limbs and neck. All the time it was working it kept up a sort of hissing whisper to itself; and when it was excited—which it usually was—the end of its nose wrinkled like a rabbit's. At last it gave another startling leap, landed ten yards away from its work, and said:

'Yes, yes. Not so good as I hoped. Do better another time. Leave it now. Come and see yourself.'

Ransom obeyed. He saw a picture of the planets, not now arranged to make a map of the solar system, but advancing in a single procession towards the spectator, and all, save one, bearing its fiery charioteer. Below lay Malacandra and there, to his surprise, was a very tolerable picture of the space-ship. Beside it stood three figures for all of which Ransom had apparently been the model. He recoiled from them in disgust. Even allowing for the strangeness of the subject from a Malacandrian point of view and for the stylization of their art, still, he thought, the creature might have made a better attempt at the human form than these stocklike dummies, almost as thick as they were tall, and sprouting about the head and neck into something that looked like fungus.

He hedged. 'I expect it is like me as I look to your people,' he said. 'It is not how they would draw me in my own world.'

'No,' said the *pfifltrigg*. 'I do not mean it to be too like. Too like, and they will not believe it—those who are born after.' He added a good deal more which was difficult to understand; but while he was speaking it dawned upon Ransom that the odious figures were intended as an *idealization* of humanity. Conversation languished for a little. To change the subject Ransom asked a question which had been in his mind for some time.

'I cannot understand,' he said, 'how you and the *sorns* and the *hrossa* all come to speak the same speech. For your tongues and teeth and throats must be very different.'

'You are right,' said the creature. 'Once we all had different speeches and we still have at home. But everyone has learned the speech of the *hrossa*.'

'Why is that?' said Ransom, still thinking in terms of terrestrial history. 'Did the *hrossa* once rule the others?'

'I do not understand. They are our great speakers and singers. They have more words and better. No one learns the speech of my people, for what we have to say is said in stone and suns' blood and stars' milk and all can see them. No one learns the *sorns'* speech, for you can change their knowledge into any words and it is still the same. You cannot do that with the songs of the *hrossa*. Their tongue goes all over Malacandra. I speak it to you because you are a stranger. I would speak it to a *sorn*. But we have our old tongues at home. You can see it in the names. The *sorns* have big-sounding names like Augray and Arkal and Belmo and Falmay. The *hrossa* have furry names like Hnoh and Hnihi and Hyoi and Hlithnahi.'

'The best poetry, then, comes in the roughest speech?'

'Perhaps,' said the *pfifltrigg*. 'As the best pictures are made in the hardest stone. But my people have names like Kalakaperi and Parakataru and Tafalakeruf. I am called Kanakaberaka.'

Ransom told it his name.

'In our country,' said Kanakaberaka, 'it is not like this. We are not pinched in a narrow *handramit*. There are the true forests, the green shadows, the deep mines. It is warm. It does not blaze with light like this, and it is not silent like this. I could put you in a place there in the forests where you could see a hundred fires at once and hear a hundred hammers. I wish you had come to our country. We do not live in holes like the *sorns* nor in bundles of weed like the *hrossa*. I could show you houses with a hundred pillars, one suns' blood and the next of stars' milk, all the way . . . and all the world painted on the walls.'

'How do you rule yourselves?' asked Ransom. 'Those who are digging in the mines—do they like it as much as those who paint the walls?'

'All keep the mines open; it is a work to be shared. But each digs for himself the thing he wants for his work. What else would he do?'

'It is not so with us.'

'Then you must make very bent work. How would a maker understand working in suns' blood unless he went into the home of suns' blood himself and knew one kind from another and lived with it for days out of the light of the sky till it was in his blood and his heart, as if he thought it and ate it and spat it?'

'With us it lies very deep and hard to get and those who dig it must spend their whole lives on the skill.'

'And they love it?'

'I think not . . . I do not know. They are kept at it because they are given no food if they stop.'

Kanakaberaka wrinkled his nose. 'Then there is not food in plenty on your world?'

'I do not know,' said Ransom. 'I have often wished to know the answer to that question but no one can tell me. Does no one keep your people at their work, Kanakaberaka?'

'Our females,' said the *pfifltrigg* with a piping noise which was apparently his equivalent for a laugh.

'Are your females of more account among you than those of the other *hnau* among them?'

'Very greatly. The *sorns* make least account of females and we make most.'

## Chapter 18

THAT NIGHT Ransom slept in the guest-house, which was a real house built by *pfifltriggi* and richly decorated. His pleasure at finding himself, in this respect, under more human conditions was qualified by the discomfort which, despite his reason, he could not help feeling in the presence, at close quarters, of so many Malacandrian creatures. All three species were represented. They seemed to have no uneasy feelings towards each other, though there were some differences of the kind that occur in a railway carriage on Earth—the *sorns* finding the house too hot and the *pfifltriggi* finding it too cold. He learned more of Malacandrian humour and of the noises that expressed it in this one night than he had learned during the whole of his life on the strange planet hitherto. Indeed, nearly all Malacandrian conversations in which he had yet taken part had been grave. Apparently the comic spirit arose chiefly from the meeting of the different kinds of *hnau*. The jokes of all three were equally incomprehensible to him. He thought he could see differences in kind—as that the *sorns* seldom got beyond irony, while the *hrossa* were extravagant and fantastic, and the *pfifltriggi* were sharp and excelled in abuse—but even when he understood all the words he could not see the points. He went early to bed.

It was at the time of early morning, when men on Earth go out to milk the cows, that Ransom was awakened. At first he did not know what had roused him. The chamber in which he lay was silent, empty and nearly dark. He was preparing himself to sleep again when a high-pitched voice close beside him said, 'Oyarsa sends for you.' He sat up, staring about him. There was no one there, and the voice repeated, 'Oyarsa sends for you.' The confusion of sleep was now clearing in his head, and he recognized that there was an *eldil* in the room. He felt no conscious fear, but while he rose obediently and put on such of his clothes as he had laid aside he found that his heart was beating rather fast. He was thinking less of the invisible creature in the room than of the interview that

117

lay before him. His old terrors of meeting some monster or idol had quite left him: he felt nervous as he remembered feeling on the morning of an examination when he was an undergraduate. More than anything in the world he would have liked a cup of good tea.

The guest-house was empty. He went out. The bluish smoke was rising from the lake and the sky was bright behind the jagged eastern wall of the canyon; it was a few minutes before sunrise. The air was still very cold, the ground-weed drenched with dew, and there was something puzzling about the whole scene which he presently identified with the silence. The *eldil* voices in the air had ceased and so had the shifting network of small lights and shades. Without being told, he knew that it was his business to go up to the crown of the island and the grove. As he approached them he saw with a certain sinking of heart that the monolithic avenue was full of Malacandrian creatures, and all silent. They were in two lines, one on each side, and all squatting or sitting in the various fashions suitable to their anatomies. He walked on slowly and doubt-fully, not daring to stop, and ran the gauntlet of all those inhuman and unblinking eyes. When he had come to the very summit, at the middle of the avenue where the biggest of the stones rose, he stopped—he never could remember afterwards whether an *eldil* voice had told him to do so or whether it was an intuition of his own. He did not sit down, for the earth was too cold and wet and he was not sure if it would be decorous. He simply stood—motionless like a man on parade. All the creatures were looking at him and there was no noise anywhere.

He perceived, gradually, that the place was full of *eldila*. The lights, or suggestions of light, which yesterday had been scattered over the island, were now all congregated in this one spot, and were all stationary or very faintly moving. The sun had risen by now, and still no one spoke. As he looked up to see the first, pale sunlight upon the monoliths, he became conscious that the air above him was full of a far greater complexity of light than the sunrise could explain, and light of a different kind, *eldil*-light. The sky, no less than the earth, was full of them; the visible Malacandrians were but the smallest part of the silent consistory which surrounded him.

He might, when the time came, be pleading his cause before thousands or before millions: rank behind rank about him, and rank above rank over his head, the creatures that had never yet seen man, and whom man could not see, were waiting for his trial to begin. He licked his lips, which were quite dry, and wondered if he would be able to speak when speech was demanded of him. Then it occurred to him that perhaps this—this waiting and being looked at—*was* the trial; perhaps even now he was unconsciously telling them all they wished to know. But afterwards—a long time afterwards— there was a noise of movement. Every visible creature in the grove had risen to its feet and was standing, more hushed than ever, with its head bowed; and Ransom saw (if it could be called seeing) that Oyarsa was coming up between the long lines of sculptured stones. Partly he knew it from the faces of the Malacandrians as their lord passed them; partly he saw—he could not deny that he saw—Oyarsa himself. He never could say what it was like. The merest whisper of light —no, less than that, the smallest diminution of shadow— was travelling along the uneven surface of the ground-weed; or rather some difference in the look of the ground, too slight to be named in the language of the five senses, moved slowly towards him. Like a silence spreading over a room full of people, like an infinitesimal coolness on a sultry day, like a passing memory of some long-forgotten sound or scent, like all that is stillest and smallest and most hard to seize in nature, Oyarsa passed between his subjects and drew near and came to rest, not ten yards away from Ransom in the centre of Meldilorn. Ransom felt a tingling of his blood and a pricking on his fingers as if lightning were near him; and his heart and body seemed to him to be made of water.

Oyarsa spoke—a more unhuman voice than Ransom had yet heard, sweet and seemingly remote; an unshaken voice; a voice, as one of the *hrossa* afterwards said to Ransom, 'with no blood in it. Light is instead of blood for them.' The words were not alarming.

'What are you so afraid of, Ransom of Thulcandra?' it said.

'Of you, Oyarsa, because you are unlike me and I cannot see you.'

'Those are not great reasons,' said the voice. 'You are also unlike me, and, though I see you, I see you very faintly. But do not think we are utterly unlike. We are both copies of Maleldil. These are not the real reasons.'

Ransom said nothing.

'You began to be afraid of me before you set foot in my world. And you have spent all your time then in flying from me. My servants saw your fear when you were in your ship in heaven. They saw that your own kind treated you ill, though they could not understand their speech. Then to deliver you out of the hands of those two I stirred up a *hnakra* to try if you would come to me of your own will. But you hid among the *hrossa*, and though they told you to come to me, you would not. After that I sent my *eldil* to fetch you, but still you would not come. And in the end your own kind have chased you to me, and *hnau's* blood has been shed.'

'I do not understand, Oyarsa. Do you mean that it was you who sent for me from Thulcandra?'

'Yes. Did not the other two tell you this? And why did you come with them unless you meant to obey my call? My servants could not understand their talk to you when your ship was in heaven.'

'Your servants . . . I cannot understand,' said Ransom.

'Ask freely,' said the voice.

'Have you servants out in the heavens?'

'Where else? There is nowhere else.'

'But you, Oyarsa, are here on Malacandra, as I am.'

'But Malacandra, like all worlds, floats in heaven. And I am not "here" altogether as you are, Ransom of Thulcandra. Creatures of your kind must drop out of heaven into a world; for us the worlds are places in heaven. But do not try to understand this now. It is enough to know that I and my servants are even now in heaven; they were around you in the sky-ship no less than they are around you here.'

'Then you knew of our journey before we left Thulcandra?'

'No. Thulcandra is the world we do not know. It alone is outside the heaven, and no message comes from it.'

Ransom was silent, but Oyarsa answered his unspoken questions.

'It was not always so. Once we knew the Oyarsa of your world—he was brighter and greater than I—and then we did not call it Thulcandra. It is the longest of all stories and the bitterest. He became bent. That was before any life came on your world. Those were the Bent Years of which we still speak in the heavens, when he was not yet bound to Thulcandra but free like us. It was in his mind to spoil other worlds besides his own. He smote your moon with his left hand and with his right he brought the cold death on my *harandra* before its time; if by my arm Maleldil had not opened the *handramits* and let out the hot springs, my world would have been unpeopled. We did not leave him so at large for long. There was great war, and we drove him back out of the heavens and bound him in the air of his own world as Maleldil taught us. There doubtless he lies to this hour, and we know no more of that planet: it is silent. We think that Maleldil would not give it up utterly to the Bent One, and there are stories among us that He has taken strange counsel and dared terrible things, wrestling with the Bent One in Thulcandra. But of this we know less than you; it is a thing we desire to look into.'

It was some time before Ransom spoke again and Oyarsa respected his silence. When he had collected himself he said:

'After this story, Oyarsa, I may tell you that our world is very bent. The two who brought me knew nothing of you, but only that the *sorns* had asked for me. They thought you were a false *eldil*, I think. There are false *eldila* in the wild parts of our world; men kill other men before them—they think the *eldil* drinks blood. They thought the *sorns* wanted me for this or for some other evil. They brought me by force. I was in terrible fear. The tellers of tales in our world make us think that if there is any life beyond our own air it is evil.'

'I understand,' said the voice. 'And this explains things that I have wondered at. As soon as your journey had passed your own air and entered heaven, my servants told me that you seemed to be coming unwillingly and that the others had secrets from you. I did not think any creature could be so bent as to bring another of its own kind here by force.'

'They did not know what you wanted me for, Oyarsa. Nor do I know yet.'

'I will tell you. Two years ago—and that is about four of your years—this ship entered the heavens from your world.

We followed its journey all the way hither and *eldila* were with it as it sailed over the *harandra,* and when at last it came to rest in the *handramit* more than half my servants were standing round it to see the strangers come out. All beasts we kept back from the place, and no *hnau* yet knew of it. When the strangers had walked to and fro on Malacandra and made themselves a hut and their fear of a new world ought to have worn off, I sent certain *sorns* to show themselves and to teach the strangers our language. I chose *sorns* because they are most like your people in form. The Thulcandrians feared the *sorns* and were very unteachable. The *sorns* went to them many times and taught them a little. They reported to me that the Thulcandrians were taking suns' blood wherever they could find it in the streams. When I could make nothing of them by report, I told the *sorns* to bring them to me, not by force but courteously. They would not come. I asked for one of them, but not even one of them would come. It would have been easy to take them; but though we saw they were stupid we did not know yet how bent they were, and I did not wish to stretch my authority beyond the creatures of my own world. I told the *sorns* to treat them like cubs, to tell them that they would be allowed to pick up no more of the suns' blood until one of their race came to me. When they were told this they stuffed as much as they could into the sky-ship and went back to their own world. We wondered at this, but now it is plain. They thought I wanted one of your race to eat and went to fetch one. If they had come a few miles to see me I would have received them honourably; now they have twice gone a voyage of millions of miles for nothing and will appear before me none the less. And you also, Ransom of Thulcandra, you have taken many vain troubles to avoid standing where you stand now.'

'That is true, Oyarsa. Bent creatures are full of fears. But I am here now and ready to know your will with me.'

'Two things I wanted to ask of your race. First I must know why you come here—so much is my duty to my world. And secondly I wish to hear of Thulcandra and of Maleldil's strange wars there with the Bent One; for that, as I have said, is a thing we desire to look into.'

'For the first question, Oyarsa, I have come here because

I was brought. Of the others, one cares for nothing but the suns' blood, because in our world he can exchange it for many pleasures and powers. But the other means evil to you. I think he would destroy all your people to make room for our people; and then he would do the same with other worlds again. He wants our race to last for always, I think, and he hopes they will leap from world to world . . . always going to a new sun when an old one dies . . . or something like that.'

'Is he wounded in his brain?'

'I do not know. Perhaps I do not describe his thoughts right. He is more learned than I.'

'Does he think he could go to the great worlds? Does he think Maleldil wants a race to live for ever?"

'He does not know there is any Maleldil. But what is certain, Oyarsa, is that he means evil to your world. Our kind must not be allowed to come here again. If you can prevent it only by killing all three of us, I am content.'

'If you were my own people I would kill them now, Ransom, and you soon; for they are bent beyond hope, and you, when you have grown a little braver, will be ready to go to Maleldil. But my authority is over my own world. It is a terrible thing to kill someone else's *hnau*. It will not be necessary.'

'They are strong Oyarsa, and they can throw death many miles and can blow killing airs at their enemies.'

'The least of my servants could touch their ship before it reached Malacandra, while it was in the heaven, and make it a body of different movements—for you, no body at all. Be sure that no one of your race will come into my world again unless I call him. But enough of this. Now tell me of Thulcandra. Tell me all. We know nothing since the day when the Bent One sank out of heaven into the air of your world, wounded in the very light of his light. But why have you become afraid again?'

'I am afraid of the lengths of time, Oyarsa . . . or perhaps I do not understand. Did you not say this happened before there was life on Thulcandra?'

'Yes.'

'And you, Oyarsa? You have lived . . . and that picture on the stone where the cold is killing them on the *ha-*

*randra*? Is that a picture of something that was before my world began?'

'I see you are *hnau* after all,' said the voice. 'Doubtless no stone that faced the air then would be a stone now. The picture has begun to crumble away and been copied again more times than there are *eldila* in the air above us. But it was copied right. In that way you are seeing a picture that was finished when your world was still half-made. But do not think of these things. My people have a law never to speak much of sizes or numbers to you others, not even to *sorns*. You do not understand, and it makes you do reverence to nothings and pass by what is really great. Rather tell me what Maleldil has done in Thulcandra.'

'According to our traditions——' Ransom was beginning, when an unexpected disturbance broke in upon the solemn stillness of the assembly. A large party, almost a procession, was approaching the grove from the direction of the ferry. It consisted entirely, as far as he could see, of *hrossa*, and they appeared to be carrying something.

# Chapter 19

AS THE PROCESSION drew nearer Ransom saw that the foremost *hrossa* were supporting three long and narrow burdens. They carried them on their heads, four *hrossa* to each. After these came a number of others armed with harpoons and apparently guarding two creatures which he did not recognize. The light was behind them as they entered between the two farthest monoliths. They were much shorter than any animal he had yet seen on Malacandra, and he gathered that they were bipeds, though the lower limbs were so thick and sausage-like that he hesitated to call them legs. The bodies were a little narrower at the top than at the bottom so as to be very slightly pear-shaped, and the heads were neither round like those of *hrossa* nor long like those of *sorns*, but almost square. They stumped along on narrow, heavy-looking feet which they seemed to press into the ground with unnecessary violence. And now their faces were becoming visible as masses of lumped and puckered flesh of variegated colour fringed in some bristly, dark substance. . . . Suddenly, with an indescribable change of feeling, he realized that he was looking at men. The two prisoners were Weston and Devine and he, for one privileged moment, had seen the human form with almost Malacandrian eyes.

The leaders of the procession had now advanced to within a few yards of Oyarsa and laid down their burdens. These, he now saw, were three dead *hrossa* laid on biers of some unknown metal; they were on their backs and their eyes, not closed as we close the eyes of human dead, stared disconcertingly up at the far-off golden canopy of the grove. One of them he took to be Hyoi, and it was certainly Hyoi's brother, Hyahi, who now came forward, and after an obeisance to Oyarsa began to speak.

Ransom at first did not hear what he was saying, for his attention was concentrated on Weston and Devine. They were weaponless and vigilantly guarded by the armed *hrossa* about them. Both of them, like Ransom himself, had let their beards grow ever since they landed on Malacandra, and both were pale and travel-stained. Weston was standing with folded arms, and his face wore a fixed, even an elaborate, expression of desperation. Devine, with his hands in his pockets, seemed to be in a state of furious sulks. Both clearly thought that they had good reason to fear, though neither was by any means lacking in courage. Surrounded by their guards as they were, and intent on the scene before them, they had not noticed Ransom.

He became aware of what Hyoi's brother was saying.

'For the death of these two, Oyarsa, I do not so much complain, for when we fell upon the *hmāna* by night they were in terror. You may say it was as a hunt and these two were killed as they might have been by a *hnakra*. But Hyoi they hit from afar with a coward's weapon when he had done nothing to frighten them. And now he lies there (and I do not say it because he was my brother, but all the *handramit* knows it) and he was a *hnak-rapunt* and a great poet and the loss of him is heavy.'

The voice of Oyarsa spoke for the first time to the two men.

'Why have you killed my *hnau*?' it said.

Weston and Devine looked anxiously about them to identify the speaker.

'God!' exclaimed Devine in English. 'Don't tell me they've got a loud-speaker.'

'Ventriloquism,' replied Weston in a husky whisper. 'Quite common among savages. The witch-doctor or medicine-man pretends to go into a trance and he does it. The thing to do is to identify the medicine-man and address your remarks to *him* wherever the voice seems to come from; it shatters his nerve and shows you've seen through him. Do you see any of the brutes in a trance? By jove—I've spotted him.'

Due credit must be given to Weston for his powers of observation: he had picked out the only creature in the assembly which was not standing in an attitude of reverence and attention. This was an elderly *hross* close beside him. It was squatting; and its eyes were shut. Taking a step towards it, he struck a defiant attitude and exclaimed in a loud voice (his knowledge of the language was elementary):

'Why you take our puff-bangs away? We very angry with you. We not afraid.'

On Weston's hypothesis his action ought to have been impressive. Unfortunately for him, no one else shared his theory of the elderly *hross's* behavior. The *hross*—who was well known to all of them, including Ransom—had not come with the funeral procession. It had been in its place since dawn. Doubtless it intended no disrespect to Oyarsa; but it must be confessed that it had yielded, at a much earlier stage of the proceedings, to an infirmity which attacks elderly *hnau* of all species, and was by this time enjoying a profound and refreshing slumber. One of its whiskers twitched a little as Weston shouted in its face, but its eyes remained shut.

The voice of Oyarsa spoke again. 'Why do you speak to him?' it said. 'It is I who ask you. Why have you killed my *hnau?*'

'You let us go, then we talkee-talkee,' bellowed Weston at the sleeping *hross*. 'You think we no power, think you do all you like. You no can. Great big head-man in sky he send us. You no do what I say, he come, blow you all up—Pouff! Bang!'

'I do not know what *bang* means,' said the voice. 'But why have you killed my *hnau?*'

'Say it was an accident,' muttered Devine to Weston in English.

'I've told you before,' replied Weston in the same language. 'You don't understand how to deal with natives. One sign of yielding and they'll be at our throats. The only thing is to intimidate them.'

'All right! Do your stuff, then,' growled Devine. He was obviously losing faith in his partner.

Weston cleared his throat and again rounded on the elderly *hross*.

'We kill him,' he shouted. 'Show what we can do. Every one who no do all we say—pouff! bang!—kill him same as that one. You do all we say and we give you much pretty things. See! See!' To Ransom's intense discomfort, Weston at this point whipped out of his pocket a brightly coloured necklace of beads, the undoubted work of Mr. Woolworth, and began dangling it in front of the faces of his guards, turning slowly round and round and repeating, 'Pretty, pretty! See! See!'

The result of this manœuvre was more striking than Weston himself had anticipated. Such a roar of sounds as human ears had never heard before—baying of *hrossa*, piping of *pfifltriggi*, booming of *sorns*—burst out and rent the silence of that august place, waking echoes from the distant mountain walls. Even in the air above them there was a faint ringing of the *eldil* voices. It is greatly to Weston's credit that though he paled at this he did not lose his nerve.

'You no roar at me,' he thundered. 'No try make me afraid. Me no afraid of you.'

'You must forgive my people,' said the voice of Oyarsa—and even it was subtly changed—'but they are not roaring at you. They are only laughing.'

But Weston did not know the Malacandrian word for *laugh*: indeed, it was not a word he understood very well in any language. He looked about him with a puzzled expression. Ransom, biting his lips with mortification, almost prayed that one experiment with the beads would satisfy the scientist; but that was because he did not know Weston. The latter saw that the clamour had subsided. He knew that he was following the most orthodox rules for frightening and then conciliating primitive races; and he was not the man to be deterred by one or two failures. The roar that went up from the throats of all spectators as he again began revolving like a slow-motion picture of a humming-top, occasionally mopping his brow with his left hand and conscientiously jerking the necklace up and down with his right, completely drowned anything he might be attempting to say; but Ransom saw his lips moving and had little doubt that he was working away at 'Pretty, pretty!' Then suddenly the sound of laughter almost redoubled its volume. The stars in their courses were fighting against Weston. Some hazy memory of efforts made long since to entertain an infant niece had begun to penetrate his highly trained mind. He was bobbing up and down from the knees and holding his head on one side; he was almost dancing; and he was by now very hot indeed. For all Ransom knew he was saying 'Diddle, diddle, diddle.'

It was sheer exhaustion which ended the great physicist's performance—the most successful of its kind ever given on Malacandra—and with it the sonorous raptures of his audience. As silence returned Ransom heard Devine's voice in English:

'For God's sake stop making a buffoon of yourself, Weston,' it said. 'Can't you see it won't work?'

'It *doesn't* seem to be working,' admitted Weston, 'and I'm inclined to think they have even less intelligence than we supposed. Do you think, perhaps, if I tried it just once again— or would you like to try this time?'

'Oh, Hell!' said Devine, and, turning his back on his partner, sat down abruptly on the ground, produced his cigarette-case and began to smoke.

'I'll give it to the witch-doctor,' said Weston during the moment of silence which Devine's action had produced among the mystified spectators; and before anyone could stop him he took a step forward and attempted to drop the string of beads round the elderly *hross's* neck. The *hross's* head was, however, too large for this operation and the necklace merely settled on its forehead like a crown, slightly over one eye. It shifted its head a little, like a dog worried with flies, snorted gently, and resumed its sleep.

Oyarsa's voice now addressed Ransom. 'Are your fellow-creatures hurt in their brains, Ransom of Thulcandra?' it said. 'Or are they too much afraid to answer my questions?'

'I think, Oyarsa,' said Ransom, 'that they do not believe you are there. And they believe that all these *hnau* are—are like very young cubs. The thicker *hmān* is trying to frighten them and then to please them with gifts.'

At the sound of Ransom's voice the two prisoners turned sharply around. Weston was about to speak when Ransom interrupted him hastily in English:

'Listen, Weston. It is not a trick. There really is a creature there in the middle—there where you can see a kind of light, or a kind of something, if you look hard. And it is at least as intelligent as a man—they seem to live an enormous time. Stop treating it like a child and answer its questions. And if you take my advice, you'll speak the truth and not bluster.'

'The brutes seem to have intelligence enough to take you in, anyway,' growled Weston; but it was in a somewhat modified voice that he turned once more to the sleeping *hross*—the desire to wake up the supposed witch-doctor was becoming an obsession—and addressed it.

'We sorry we kill him,' he said, pointing to Hyoi. 'No go to kill him. *Sorns* tell us bring man, give him your big head. We go away back into sky. *He* come (here he indicated Ransom) with us. He very bent man, run away, no do what *sorns* say like us. We run after him, get him back for *sorns*, want to do what we say and *sorns* tell us, see? He not let us. Run away, run, run. We run after. See big black one, think he kill us, we kill him—pouff! bang! All for bent man. He no run away, he be good, we no run after, no kill big black one, see? You have bent man—bent man make all trouble—you plenty keep him, let us go. He afraid of you, we no afraid. Listen——'

At this moment Weston's continual bellowing in the face of the *hross* at last produced the effect he had striven for so long. The creature opened its eyes and stared mildly at him in some perplexity. Then, gradually realizing the impropriety of which it had been guilty, it rose slowly to its standing position, bowed respectfully to Oyarsa, and finally waddled out of the assembly still carrying the necklace draped over its right ear and eye. Weston, his mouth still open, followed the retreating figure with his gaze till it vanished among the stems of the grove.

It was Oyarsa who broke the silence. 'We have had mirth enough,' he said, 'and it is time to hear true answers to our questions. Something is wrong in your head, *hnau* from Thulcandra. There is too much blood in it. Is Firikitekila here?'

'Here, Oyarsa,' said a *pfifltrigg*.

'Have you in your cisterns water that has been made cold?'

'Yes, Oyarsa.'

'Then let this thick *hnau* be taken to the guest-house and let them bathe his head in cold water. Much water and many times. Then bring him again. Meanwhile I will provide for my killed *hrossa*.'

Weston did not clearly understand what the voice said—indeed, he was still too busy trying to find out where it came from—but terror smote him as he found himself wrapped in the strong arms of the surrounding *hrossa* and forced away from his place. Ransom would gladly have shouted out some reassurance, but Weston himself was shouting too loud to hear him. He was mixing English and Malacandrian now, and the last that was heard was a rising scream of 'Pay for this—pouff! bang!—Ransom, for God's sake—Ransom! Ransom!'

'And now,' said Oyarsa, when silence was restored, 'let us honour my dead *hnau*.'

At his words ten of the *hrossa* grouped themselves about the biers. Lifting their heads, and with no signal given as far as Ransom could see, they began to sing.

To every man, in his acquaintance with a new art, there comes a moment when that which before was meaningless first lifts, as it were, one corner of the curtain that hides its mystery, and reveals, in a burst of delight which later and fuller understanding can hardly ever equal, one glimpse of the indefinite possibilities within. For Ransom, this moment had now come in his understanding of Malacandrian song. Now first he saw that its rhythms were based on a different blood from ours, on a heart that beat more quickly, and a fiercer internal heat. Through his knowledge of the creatures and his love for them he began, ever to little, to hear it with their ears. A sense of great masses moving at visionary speeds, of giants dancing, of eternal sorrows eternally consoled, of he knew not what and yet what he had always known, awoke in him with the very first bars of the deep-mouthed dirge, and bowed down his spirit as if the gate of heaven had opened before him.

'Let it go hence,' they sang. 'Let it go hence, dissolve and be no body. Drop it, release it, drop it gently, as a stone is loosed from the fingers drooping over a still pool. Let it go down, sink, fall away. Once below the surface there are no divisions, no layers in the water yielding all the way down; all one and all unwounded is that element. Send it voyaging where it will not come again. Let it go down; the *hnau* rises from it. This is the second life, the other beginning. Open, oh coloured world, without weight, without shore. You are second and better; this was first and feeble. Once the worlds were hot within and brought forth life, but only the pale plants, the dark plants. We see their children when they grow to-day, out of the sun's light in the sad places. After, the heaven made grow another kind on worlds: the high climbers, the bright-haired forests, cheeks of flowers. First were the darker, then the brighter. First was the worlds' blood, then the suns' brood.'

This was as much of it as he contrived later to remember and could translate. As the song ended Oyarsa said:

'Let us scatter the movements which were their bodies. So will Maleldil scatter all worlds when the first and feeble is worn.'

He made a sign to one of the *pfifltriggi*, who instantly arose and approached the corpses. The *hrossa*, now singing again but very softly, drew back at least ten paces. The *pfifltrigg* touched each of the three dead in turn with some small object that appeared to be made of glass or crystal—and then jumped away with one of his frog-like leaps. Ransom closed his eyes to protect them from a blinding light and felt something like a very strong wind blowing in his face, for a fraction of a second. Then all was calm again, and the three biers were empty.

'God! That would be a trick worth knowing on earth,' said Devine to Ransom. 'Solves the murderers' problem about the disposal of the body, eh?'

But Ransom, who was thinking of Hyoi, did not answer him; and before he spoke again everyone's attention was diverted by the return of the unhappy Weston among his guards.

# Chapter 20

THE *hross* who headed this procession was a conscientious creature and began at once explaining itself in a rather troubled voice.

'I hope we have done right, Oyarsa,' it said. 'But we do not know. We dipped his head in the cold water seven times, but the seventh time something fell off it. We had thought it was the top of his head, but now we saw it was a covering made of the skin of some other creature. Then some said we had done your will with the seven dips, and others said not. In the end we dipped it seven times more. We hope that was right. The creature talked a lot between the dips, and most between the second seven, but we could not understand it.'

'You have done very well, Hnoo,' said Oyarsa. 'Stand away that I may see it, for now I will speak to it.'

The guards fell away on each side. Weston's usually pale face, under the bracing influence of the cold water, had assumed the colour of a ripe tomato, and his hair, which had naturally not been cut since he reached Malacandra, was plastered in straight, lank masses across his forehead. A good deal of water was still dripping over his nose and ears. His expression—unfortunately wasted on an audience ignorant of terrestrial physiognomy—was that of a brave man suffering in a great cause, and rather eager than reluctant to face the worst or even to provoke it. In explanation of his conduct it is only fair to remember that he had already that morning endured all the terrors of an expected martyrdom and all the anticlimax of fourteen compulsory cold douches. Devine, who knew his man, shouted out to Weston in English:

'Steady, Weston. These devils can split the atom or something pretty like it. Be careful what you say to them and don't let's have any of your bloody nonsense.'

'Huh!' said Weston. 'So you've gone native too?'

'Be silent,' said the voice of Oyarsa. 'You, thick one, have told me nothing of yourself, so I will tell it to you. In your own world you have attained great wisdom concerning bodies and by this you have been able to make a ship that can cross the heaven; but in all other things you have the mind of an animal. When first you came here, I sent for you, meaning you nothing but honour. The darkness in your own mind filled you with fear. Because you thought I meant evil to you, you went as a beast goes against a beast of some other kind, and snared this Ransom. You would give him up to the evil you feared. To-day, seeing him here, to save your own life, you would have given him to me a second time, still thinking I meant him hurt. These are your dealings with your own kind. And what you intend to my people, I know. Already you have killed some. And you have come here to kill them all. To you it is nothing whether a creature is *hnau* or not. At first I thought this was because you cared only whether a creature had a body like your own; but Ransom has that and you would kill him as lightly as any of my *hnau*. I did not know that the Bent One had done so much in your world and still I do not understand it. If you were mine, I would unbody you even now. Do not think follies; by my hand Maleldil does greater things than this, and I can unmake you even on the borders of your own world's air. But I do not yet resolve to do this. It is for you to speak. Let me see if there is anything in your mind besides fear and death and desire.'

Weston turned to Ransom. 'I see,' he said, 'that you have chosen the most momentous crisis in the history of the human race to betray it.' Then he turned in the direction of the voice.

'I know you kill us,' he said. 'Me not afraid. Others come, make it our world——'

But Devine had jumped to his feet, and interrupted him.

'No, no Oyarsa,' he shouted. 'You no listen him. He very foolish man, he have dreams. We little people, only want pretty sun-bloods. You give us plenty sun-bloods, we go back into sky, you never see us no more. All done, see?'

'Silence,' said Oyarsa. There was an almost imperceptible change in the light, if it could be called light, out of which the voice came, and Devine crumpled up and fell back on the ground. When he resumed his sitting position he was white and panting.

'Speak on,' said Oyarsa to Weston.

'Me no . . . no,' began Weston in Malacandrian and then

broke off. 'I can't say what I want in their accursed language,' he said in English.

'Speak to Ransom and he shall turn it into our speech,' said Oyarsa.

Weston accepted the arrangement at once. He believed that the hour of his death was come and he was determined to utter the thing—almost the only thing outside his own science—which he had to say. He cleared his throat, almost he struck a gesture, and began:

'To you I may seem a vulgar robber, but I bear on my shoulders the destiny of the human race. Your tribal life with its stone-age weapons and bee-hive huts, its primitive coracles and elementary social structure, has nothing to compare with our civilization—with our science, medicine and law, our armies, our architecture, our commerce, and our transport system which is rapidly annihilating space and time. Our right to supersede you is the right of the higher over the lower. Life——'

'Half a moment,' said Ransom in English. 'That's about as much as I can manage at one go.' Then, turning to Oyarsa, he began translating as well as he could. The process was difficult and the result—which he felt to be rather unsatisfactory—was something like this:

'Among us, Oyarsa, there is a kind of *hnau* who will take other *hnau's* food and—and things, when they are not looking. He says he is not an ordinary one of that kind. He says what he does now will make very different things happen to those of our people who are not yet born. He says that, among you, *hnau* of one kindred all live together and the *hrossa* have spears like those we used a very long time ago and your huts are small and round and your boats small and light and like our old ones, and you have only one ruler. He says it is different with us. He says we know much. There is a thing happens in our world when the body of a living creature feels pains and becomes weak, and he says we sometimes know how to stop it. He says we have many bent people and we kill them or shut them in huts and that we have people for settling quarrels between the bent *hnau* about their huts and mates and things. He says we have many ways for the *hnau* of one land to kill those of another and some are trained to do it. He says we build very big and strong huts of stones and other things—like the *pfifltriggi*. And he says we exchange many things among ourselves and can carry heavy weights very quickly a long way. Because of all this, he says it would not be the act of a bent *hnau* if our people killed all your people.'

As soon as Ransom finished, Weston continued.

'Life is greater than any system of morality; her claims are absolute. It is not by tribal taboos and copy-book maxims that she has pursued her relentless march from the amœba to man and from man to civilization.'

'He says,' began Ransom, 'that living creatures are stronger than the question whether an act is bent or good—no, that cannot be right—he says it is better to be alive and bent than to be dead—no—he says, he says—I cannot say what he says, Oyarsa, in your language. But he goes on to say that the only good thing is that there should be very many creatures alive. He says there were many other animals before the first men and the later ones were better than the earlier ones; but he says the animals were not born because of what is said to the young about bent and good action by their elders. And he says these animals did not feel any pity.'

'She——' began Weston.

'I'm sorry,' interrupted Ransom, 'but I've forgotten who She is.'

'Life, of course,' snapped Weston. 'She has ruthlessly broken down all obstacles and liquidated all failures and to-day in her highest form—civilized man—and in me as his representative, she presses forward to that interplanetary leap which will, perhaps, place her for ever beyond the reach of death.'

'He says,' resumed Ransom, 'that these animals learned to do many difficult things, except those who could not; and those ones died and the other animals did not pity them. And he says the best animal now is the kind of man who makes the big huts and carries the heavy weights and does all the other things I told you about; and he is one of these and he says that if the others all knew what he was doing they would be pleased. He says that if he could kill you all and bring our people to live in Malacandra, then they might be able to go on living here after something had gone wrong with our world. And then if something went wrong with Malacandra they might go and kill all the *hnau* in another world. And then another—and so they would never die out.'

'It is in her right,' said Weston, 'the right, or, if you will, the might of Life herself, that I am prepared without flinching to plant the flag of man on the soil of Malacandra: to march on, step by step, superseding, where necessary, the lower forms of life that we find, claiming planet after planet, system after system, till our posterity—whatever strange form and yet unguessed mentality they have assumed—dwell in the universe wherever the universe is habitable.'

'He says,' translated Ransom, 'that because of this it would *not* be a bent action—or else, he says, it *would* be a possible action— for him to kill you all and bring us here. He says he would feel no pity. He is saying again that perhaps they would be able to keep moving from one world to another and wherever they came they would kill everyone. I think he is now talking about worlds that go round other suns. He wants the creatures born from us to be in as many places as they can. He says he does not know what kind of creatures they will be.'

'I may fall,' said Weston. 'But while I live I will not, with such a key in my hand, consent to close the gates of the future on my race. What lies in that future, beyond our present ken, passes imagination to conceive: it is enough for me that there is a Beyond.'

'He is saying,' Ransom translated, 'that he will not stop trying to do all this unless you kill him. And he says that though he doesn't know what will happen to the creatures sprung from us, he wants it to happen very much.'

Weston, who had now finished his statement, looked round instinctively for a chair to sink into. On Earth he usually sank into a chair as the applause began. Finding none—he was not the kind of man to sit on the ground like Devine—he folded his arm and stared with a certain dignity about him.

'It is well that I have heard you,' said Oyarsa. 'For though your mind is feebler, your will is less bent than I thought. It is not for yourself that you would do all this.'

'No,' said Weston proudly in Malacandrian. 'Me die. Man live.'

'Yet you know that these creatures would have to be made quite unlike you before they lived on other worlds.'

'Yes, yes. All new. No one know yet. Strange! Big!'

'Then it is not the shape of body that you love?'

'No. Me no care how they shaped.'

'One would think, then, that it is for the mind you care. But that cannot be, or you would love *hnau* wherever you met it.'

'No care for *hnau*. Care for man.'

'But if it is neither man's mind, which is as the mind of all other *hnau*—is not Maleldil maker of them all?—nor his body, which will change—if you care for neither of these, what do you mean by man?'

This had to be translated to Weston. When he understood it, he replied:

'Me care for man—care for our race—what man begets—' He had to ask Ransom the words for *race* and *beget*.

'Strange!' said Oyarsa. 'You do not love any one of your race—you would have let me kill Ransom. You do not love the mind of your race, nor the body. Any kind of creature will please you if only it is begotten by your kind as they now are. It seems to me, Thick One, that what you really love is no completed creature but the very seed itself: for that is all that is left.'

'Tell him,' said Weston when he had been made to understand this, 'that I don't pretend to be a metaphysician. I have not come here to chop logic. If he cannot understand—as apparently you can't either—anything so fundamental as a man's loyalty to humanity, I can't make him understand it.'

But Ransom was unable to translate this and the voice of Oyarsa continued:

'I see now how the lord of the silent world has bent you. There are laws that all *hnau* know, of pity and straight dealing and shame and the like, and one of these is the love of kindred. He has taught you to break all of them except this one, which is not one of the greatest laws; this one he has bent till it becomes folly and has set it up, thus bent, to be a little, blind Oyarsa in your brain. And now you can do nothing but obey it, though if we ask you why it is a law you give no other reason for it than for all the other and greater laws which it drives you to disobey. Do you know why he has done this?'

'Me think no such person—me wise, new man—no believe all that old talk.'

'I will tell you. He has left you this one because a bent *hnau* can do more evil than a broken one. He has only bent you; but this Thin One who sits on the ground he has broken, for he has left him nothing but greed. He is now only a talking animal and in my world he could do no more evil than an animal. If he were mine I would unmake his body for the *hnau* in it is already dead. But if you were mine I would try to cure you. Tell me, Thick One, why did you come here?'

'Me tell you. Make man live all the time.'

'But are your wise men so ignorant as not to know that Malacandra is older than your own world and nearer its death? Most of it is dead already. My people live only in the *handramits;* the heat and the water have been more and will be less. Soon now, very soon, I will end my world and give back my people to Maleldil.'

'Me know all that plenty. This only first try. Soon they go on another world.'

'But do you not know that all worlds will die?'

'Men go jump off each before it deads—on and on, see?'

'And when all are dead?'

Weston was silent. After a time Oyarsa spoke again.

'Do you not ask **why my** people, whose world is old, have not rather come to yours and taken it long ago?'

'Ho! Ho!' said Weston. 'You not know how.'

'You are wrong,' said Oyarsa. 'Many thousands of thousand years before this, when nothing yet lived on your world, the cold death was coming on my *harandra.* Then I was in deep trouble, not chiefly for the death of my *hnau*—Maleldil does not make them long-livers—but for the things which the lord of your world, who was not yet bound, put into their minds. He would have made them as your people are now—wise enough to see the death of their kind approaching but not wise enough to endure it. Bent counsels would soon have risen among them. They were well able to have made sky-ships. By me Maleldil stopped them. Some I cured, some I unbodied——'

'And see what come!' interrupted Weston. 'You now very few—shut up in *handramits*—soon all die.'

'Yes,' said Oyarsa, 'but one thing we left behind us on the *harandra*: fear. And with fear, murder and rebellion. The weakest of my people does not fear death. It is the Bent One, the lord of your world, who wastes your lives and befouls them with flying from what you know will overtake you in the end. If you were subjects of Maleldil you would have peace.'

Weston writhed in the exasperation born of his desire to speak and his ignorance of the language.

'Trash! Defeatist trash!' he shouted at Oyarsa in English; then, drawing himself up to his full height, he added in Malacandrian, 'You say your Maleldil let all go dead. Other one, Bent One, he fight, jump, live—not all talkee-talkee. Me no care Maleldil. Like Bent One better: me on his side.'

'But do you not see that he never will nor can,' began Oyarsa, and then broke off, as if recollecting himself. 'But I must learn more of your world from Ransom, and for that I need till night. I will not kill you, not even the Thin One, for you are out of my world. To-morrow you shall go hence again in your ship.'

Devine's face suddenly fell. He began talking rapidly in English.

'For God's sake, Weston, make him understand. We've been here for months—the Earth is not in opposition now. Tell him it can't be done. He might as well kill us at once.'

'How long will your journey be to Thulcandra?' asked Oyarsa.

Weston, using Ransom as his interpreter, explained that the journey, in the present position of the two planets, was almost impossible. The distance had increased by millions of miles. The angle of their course to the solar rays would be totally different from that which he had counted upon. Even if by a hundreth chance they could hit the Earth, it was almost certain that their supply of oxygen would be exhausted long before they arrived.

'Tell him to kill us now,' he added.

"All this I know,' said Oyarsa. 'And if you stay in my world I must kill you: no such creature will I suffer in Malacandra.

I know there is small chance of your reaching your world; but small is not the same as none. Between now and the next moon choose which you will take. In the meantime, tell me this. If you reach it at all, what is the most time you will need?'

After a prolonged calculation, Weston, in a shaken voice, replied that if they had not made it in ninety days they would never make it, and they would, moreover, be dead of suffocation.

'Ninety days you shall have,' said Oyarsa. 'My *sorns* and *pfifltriggi* will give you air (we also have that art) and food for ninety days. But they will do something else to your ship. I am not minded that it should return into the heaven if once it reaches Thulcandra. You, Thick One, were not here when I unmade my dead *hrossa* whom you killed: the Thin One will tell you. This I can do, as Maleldil has taught me, over a gap of time or a gap of place. Before your sky-ship rises, my *sorns* will have so dealt with it that on the ninetieth day it will unbody, it will become what you call nothing. If that day finds it in heaven your death will be no bitterer because of this; but do not tarry in your ship if once you touch Thulcandra. Now lead these two away, and do you, my children, go where you will. But I must talk with Ransom.'

## Chapter 21

ALL THAT AFTERNOON Ransom remained alone answering Oyarsa's questions. I am not allowed to record this conversation, beyond saying that the voice concluded it with the words:

'You have shown me more wonders than are known in the whole of heaven.'

After that they discussed Ransom's own future. He was given full liberty to remain in Malacandra or to attempt the desperate voyage to Earth. The problem was agonizing to him. In the end he decided to throw in his lot with Weston and Devine.

'Love of our own kind,' he said, 'is not the greatest of laws, but you, Oyarsa, have said it is a law. If I cannot live in Thulcandra, it is better for me not to live at all.'

'You have chosen rightly,' said Oyarsa. 'And I will tell you two things. My people will take all the strange weapons out of the ship, but they will give one to you. And the *eldila* of deep heaven will be about your ship till it reaches the air of Thulcandra, and often in it. They will not let the other two kill you.'

It had not occurred to Ransom before that his own murder might be one of the first expedients for economizing food and oxygen which would occur to Weston and Devine. He was now astonished at his obtuseness, and thanked Oyarsa for his protective measures. Then the great *eldil* dismissed him with these words:

'You are guilty of no evil, Ransom of Thulcandra, except a little fearfulness. For that, the journey you go on is your pain, and perhaps your cure: for you must be either mad or brave before it is ended. But I lay also a command on you; you must watch this Weston and this Devine in Thulcandra if ever you arrive there. They may yet do much evil in, and beyond, your world. From what you have told me, I begin to see that there are *eldila* who go down into your air, into the very stronghold of the Bent One; your world is not so fast shut as was thought in these parts of heaven. Watch those two bent ones. Be courageous. Fight them. And when you have need, some of our people will help. Maleldil will show them to you. It may even be that you and I shall meet again while you are still in the body; for it is not without the wisdom of Maleldil that we have met now and I have learned so much of your world. It seems to me that this is the beginning of more comings and goings between the heavens and the worlds and between one world and another—though not such as the Thick One hoped. I am allowed to tell you this. The year we are now in—but heavenly years are not as yours—has long been prophesied as a year of stirrings and high changes and the siege of Thulcandra may be near its end. Great things are on foot. If Maleldil does not forbid me, I will not hold aloof from them. And now, farewell.'

It was through vast crowds of all the Malacandrian species that the three human beings embarked next day on their terrible journey. Weston was pale and haggard from a night of calculations intricate enough to tax any mathematician even if his life did not hang on them. Devine was noisy, reckless and a little hysterical. His whole view of Malacandra had been altered overnight by the discovery that the 'natives' had an alcoholic drink, and he had even been trying to teach them to smoke. Only the *pfifltriggi* had made much of it. He was now consoling himself for an acute headache and the prospect of a lingering death by tormenting Weston. Neither partner was pleased to find that all weapons had been removed from the space-ship, but in other respects everything was as they wished it. At about an hour after noon Ransom took a last, long look at the blue waters, purple forest and remote green walls of the familiar *handramit*, and followed the other two through the manhole. Before it was closed Weston warned them that they must economize air by absolute stillness. No unnecessary movement must be made during their voyage; even talking must be prohibited.

'I shall speak only in an emergency,' he said.

'Thank God for that, anyway,' was Devine's last shot. Then they screwed themselves in.

Ransom went at once to the lower side of the sphere, into the chamber which was now most completely upside down, and stretched himself on what would later become its skylight. He was surprised to find that they were already thousands of feet up. The *handramit* was only a straight purple line across the rose-red surface of the *harandra*. They were above the junction of two *handramits*. One of them was doubtless that in which he had lived, the other that which contained Meldilorn. The gully by which he had cut off the corner between the two, on Augray's shoulders, was quite invisible.

Each minute more *handramits* came into view—long straight lines, some parallel, some intersecting, some building triangles. The landscape became increasingly geometrical. The waste between the purple lines appeared perfectly flat. The rosy colour of the petrified forests accounted for its tint immediately below him; but to the north and east the great sand deserts of which the *sorns* had told him were now appearing as illimitable stretches of yellow and ochre. To the west a huge discoloration began to show. It was an irregular patch of greenish blue that looked as if it were sunk below the level of the surrounding *harandra*. He concluded it was the forest lowland of the *pfifltriggi*—or rather one of their forest lowlands, for now similar patches were appearing in all directions, some of them mere blobs at the intersection of *handramits*, some of vast extent. He became vividly conscious that his knowledge of Malacandra was minute, local, parochial. It was as if a *sorn* had journeyed forty million miles to the Earth and spent his stay there between Worthing and Brighton. He reflected that he would have very little to show for his amazing voyage if he survived it: a smattering of the language, a few landscapes, some half-understood physics—but where were the statistics, the history, the broad survey of extra-terrestrial conditions, which such a traveller ought to bring back? Those *handramits*, for example. Seen from the height which the spaceship had now attained, in all their unmistakable geometry, they put to shame his original impression that they were natural valleys. They were gigantic feats of engineering, about which he had learned nothing; feats accomplished, if all were true, before human history began . . . before animal history began. Or was that only mythology? He knew it would seem like mythology when he got back to Earth (if he ever got back), but the presence of Oyarsa was still too fresh a memory to allow him any real doubts. It even occurred to him that the distinction ɔetween history and mythology might be itself meaningless outside the Earth.

The thought baffled him, and he turned again to the landscape below—the landscape which became every moment less of a landscape and more of a diagram. By this time, to the east, a much larger and darker patch of discoloration than he had yet seen was pushing its way into the reddish ochre of the Malacandrian world—a curiously shaped patch with long arms or horns extended on each side and a sort of bay between them, like the concave side of a crescent. It grew and grew. The wide dark arms seemed to be spread out to engulf the whole planet. Suddenly he saw a bright point of light in the middle of this dark patch and realized that it was not a patch on the surface of the planet at all, but the black sky showing behind her. The smooth curve was the edge of her disk. At this, for the first time since their embarkation, fear took hold of him. Slowly, yet not too slowly for him to see, the dark arms spread farther and even farther round the lighted surface till at last they met. The whole disk, framed in blackness, was before him. The faint percussions of the meteorites had long been audible; the window through which he was gazing was no longer definitely beneath him. His limbs, though already very light, were almost too stiff to move, and he was very hungry. He looked at his watch. He had been at his post, spell-bound, for nearly eight hours.

He made his way with difficulty to the sunward side of the ship and reeled back almost blinded with the glory of the light. Groping, he found his darkened glasses in his old cabin and got himself food and water: Weston had rationed them strictly in both. He opened the door of the control-room and looked in. Both the partners, their faces drawn with anxiety, were seated before a kind of metal table; it was covered with delicate, gently vibrating instruments in which crystal and fine wire were the predominant materials. Both ignored his presence. For the rest of the silent journey he was free of the whole ship.

When he returned to the dark side, the world they were leaving hung in the star-strewn sky not much bigger than our earthly moon. Its colours were still visible—a reddish-yellow disk blotched with greenish-blue and capped with white at the poles. He saw the two tiny Malacandrian moons—their movement quite perceptible—and reflected that they were among the thousand things he had not noticed during his sojourn there. He slept, and woke, and saw the disk still hanging in the sky. It was smaller than the Moon now. Its colours were gone except for a faint, uniform tinge of redness in its light; even the light was not now incomparably stronger than that of the countless stars which surrounded it. It had ceased to be Malacandra; it was only Mars.

He soon fell back into his old routine of sleeping and basking, punctuated with the making of some scribbled notes for his Malacandrian dictionary. He knew that there was very little chance of his being able to communicate his new knowledge to man, that unrecorded death in the depth of space would almost certainly be the end of their adventure. But already it had become impossible to think of it as 'space.' Some moments of cold fear he had; but each time they were shorter and more quickly swallowed up in a sense of awe which made his personal fate seem wholly insignificant. He could not feel that they were an island of life journeying through an abyss of death. He felt almost the opposite—that life was waiting outside the little iron egg-shell in which they rode, ready at any moment to break in, and that, if it killed them, it would kill them by excess of its vitality. He hoped passionately that if they were to perish they would perish by the 'unbodying' of the space-ship and not by suffocation within it. To be let out, to be free, to dissolve into the ocean of eternal noon, seemed to him at certain moments a consummation even more desirable than their return to Earth. And if he had felt some such lift of the heart when first he passed through heaven on their outward journey, he felt it now tenfold, for now he was convinced that the abyss was full of life in the most literal sense, full of living creatures.

His confidence in Oyarsa's words about the *eldila* increased rather than diminished as they went on. He saw none of them; the intensity of light in which the ship swam allowed none of the fugitive variations which would have betrayed their presence. But he heard, or thought he heard, all kinds of delicate sound, or vibrations akin to sound, mixed with the tinkling rain of meteorites, and often the sense of unseen presences even within the space-ship became irresistible. It was this, more than anything else, that made his own chances of life seem so unimportant. He and all his race showed small and ephemeral against a background of such immeasurable fullness. His brain reeled at the thought of the true population of the universe, the three-dimensional infinitude of their territory, and the unchronicled æons of their past; but his heart became steadier than it had ever been.

It was well for him that he had reached this frame of mind before the real hardships of their journey began. Ever since their departure from Malacandra, the thermometer had steadily risen; now it was higher than it had stood at any time on their outward journey. And it still rose. The light also increased. Under his glasses he kept his eyes habitually tight shut, opening them only for the shortest time for necessary movements. He knew that if he reached Earth it would be with permanently damaged sight. But all this was nothing to the torment of heat. All three of them were awake for twenty-four hours out of the twenty-four, enduring with dilated eyeballs, blackened lips and froth-flecked cheeks the agony of thirst. It would be madness to increase their scanty rations of water: madness even to consume air in discussing the question.

He saw well enough what was happening. In his last bid for life Weston was venturing inside the Earth's orbit, leading them nearer the Sun than man, perhaps than life, had ever been. Presumably this was unavoidable; one could not follow a retreating Earth round the rim of its own wheeling course. They must be trying to meet it—to cut across . . . it was madness! But the question did not much occupy his mind; it was not possible for long to think of anything but thirst. One thought of water; then one thought of thirst; then one thought of thinking of thirst; then of water again. And still the thermometer rose. The walls of the ship were too hot to touch. It was obvious that a crisis was approaching. In the next few hours it must kill them or get less.

It got less. There came a time when they lay exhausted and shivering in what seemed the cold, though it was still hotter than any terrestrial climate. Weston had so far succeeded; he had risked the highest temperature at which human life could theoretically survive, and they had lived through it. But they were not the same men. Hitherto Weston had slept very little even in his watches off; always, after an hour or so of uneasy rest, he had returned to his charts and to his endless, almost despairing, calculations. You could see him fighting the despair —pinning his terrified brain down, and again down, to the figures. Now he never looked at them. He even seemed careless in the control-room. Devine moved and looked like a somnambulist. Ransom lived increasingly on the dark side and for long hours he thought of nothing. Although the first great danger was past, none of them, at this time, had any serious hope of a successful issue to their journey. They had now been fifty days, without speech, in their steel shell, and the air was already very bad.

Weston was so unlike his old self that he even allowed Ransom to take his share in the navigation. Mainly by signs, but with the help of a few whispered words, he taught him all that was necessary at this stage of the journey. Apparently they were racing home—but with little chance of reaching it in time—before some sort of cosmic 'trade-wind.' A few rules of thumb enabled Ransom to keep the star which Weston pointed out to him in its position at the centre of the skylight, but always with his left hand on the bell to Weston's cabin.

This star was not the Earth. The days—the purely theoretical 'days' which bore such a desperately practical meaning for the travellers—mounted to fifty-eight before Weston changed course, and a different luminary was in the centre. Sixty days, and it was visibly a planet. Sixty-six, and it was like a planet seen through field-glasses. Seventy and it was like nothing that Ransom had ever seen—a little dazzling disk too large for a planet and far too small for the Moon. Now that he was navigating, his celestial mood was shattered. Wild, animal thirst for life, mixed with homesick longing for the free airs and the sights and smells of earth—for grass and meat and beer and tea and the human voice—awoke in him. At first his chief difficulty on watch had been to resist drowsiness; now, though the air was worse, feverish excitement kept him vigilant. Often when he came off duty he found his right arm stiff and sore; for hours he had been pressing it unconsciously against the control-board as if his puny thrust could spur the space-ship to yet greater speed.

Now they had twenty days to go. Nineteen—eighteen—and on the white terrestrial disk, now a little larger than a sixpence, he thought he could make out Australia and the southeast corner of Asia. Hour after hour, though the markings moved slowly across the disk with the Earth's diurnal revolution, the disk itself refused to grow larger. 'Get on! Get on!' Ransom muttered to the ship. Now ten days were left and it was like the Moon and so bright that they could not look steadily at it. The air in their little sphere was ominously bad, but Ransom and Devine risked a whisper as they changed watches.

'We'll do it,' they said. 'We'll do it yet.'

On the eighty-seventh day, when Ransom relieved Devine, he thought there was something wrong with the Earth. Before his watch was done, he was sure. It was no longer a true circle, but bulging a little on one side; it was almost pear-shaped. When Weston came on duty he gave one glance at the skylight, rang furiously on the bell for Devine, thrust Ransom aside, and took the navigating seat. His face was the colour of putty. He seemed to be about to do something to the controls, but as Devine entered the room he looked up and shrugged his shoulders with a gesture of despair. Then he buried his face in his hands and laid his head down on the control-board.

Ransom and Devine exchanged glances. They bundled Weston out of the seat—he was crying like a child—and Devine took his place. And now at last Ransom understood the mystery of the bulging Earth. What had appeared as a bulge on one side of her disk was becoming increasingly distinct as a second disk, a disk almost as large in appearance as her own. It was covering more than half of the Earth. It was the Moon —between them and the Earth, and two hundred and forty thousand miles nearer. Ransom did not know what fate this might mean for the space-ship. Devine obviously did, and never had he appeared so admirable. His face was as pale as Weston's, but his eyes were clear and preternaturally bright; he sat crouched over the controls like an animal about to spring and he was whistling very softly between his teeth.

Hours later Ransom understood what was happening. The Moon's disk was now larger than the Earth's and very gradually it became apparent to him that both disks were diminishing in size. The space-ship was no longer approaching either the Earth or the Moon; it was farther away from them than it had been half an hour ago, and that was the meaning of Devine's feverish activity with the controls. It was not merely that the Moon was crossing their path and cutting them off from the Earth; apparently for some reason—probably gravitational—it was dangerous to get too close to the Moon, and Devine was standing off into space. In sight of harbour they were being forced to turn back to the open sea. He glanced up at the chronometer. It was the morning of the eighty-eighth day. Two days to make the Earth, and they were moving away from her.

'I suppose this finishes us?' he whispered.

'Expect so,' whispered Devine, without looking round.

Weston presently recovered sufficiently to come back and stand beside Devine. There was nothing for Ransom to do. He was sure now, that they were soon to die. With this realization, the agony of his suspense suddenly disappeared. Death, whether it came now or some thirty years later on Earth, rose up and claimed his attention. There were preparations a man likes to make. He left the control-room and returned into one of the sunward chambers, into the indifference of the moveless light, the warmth, the silence and the sharp-cut shadows. Nothing was farther from his mind than sleep. It must have been the exhausted atmosphere which made him drowsy. He slept.

He awoke in almost complete darkness in the midst of a loud continuous noise, which he could not at first identify. It reminded him of something—something he seemed to have heard in a previous existence. It was a prolonged drumming noise close above his head. Suddenly his heart gave a great leap.

'Oh God,' he sobbed. 'Oh God! It's *rain*.'

He was on Earth. The air was heavy and stale about him, but the choking sensations he had been suffering were gone. He realized that he was still in the space-ship. The others, in fear of its threatened 'unbodying,' had characteristically abandoned it the moment it touched Earth and left him to his fate. It was difficult in the dark, and under the crushing weight of terrestrial gravity, to find his way out. But he managed it. He found the manhole and slithered, drinking great draughts of air, down the outside of the sphere; slipped in mud, blessed the smell of it, and at last raised the unaccustomed weight of his body to its feet. He stood in pitch-black night under torrential rain. With every pore of his body he drank it in; with every desire of his heart he embraced the smell of the field about him—a patch of his native planet where grass grew, where cows moved, where presently he would come to hedges and a gate.

He had walked about half an hour when a vivid light behind him and a strong, momentary wind informed him that the space-ship was no more. He felt very little interest. He had seen dim lights, the lights of men, ahead. He contrived to get into a lane, then into a road, then into a village street. A lighted door was open. There were voices from within and they were speaking English. There was a familiar smell. He pushed his way in, regardless of the surprise he was creating, and walked to the bar.

'A pint of bitter, please,' said Ransom.

## Chapter 22

AT THIS POINT, if I were guided by purely literary considerations, my story would end, but it is time to remove the mask and to acquaint the reader with the real and practical purpose for which this book has been written. At the same time he will learn how the writing of it became possible at all.

Dr. Ransom—and at this stage it will become obvious that that is not his real name—soon abandoned the idea of his Malacandrian dictionary and indeed all idea of communicating his story to the world. He was ill for several months, and when he recovered he found himself in considerable doubt as to whether what he remembered had really occurred. It looked very like a delusion produced by his illness, and most of his apparent adventures could, he saw, be explained psychoanalytically. He did not lean very heavily on this fact himself, for he had long since observed that a good many 'real' things in the fauna and flora of our own world could be accounted for in the same way if you started with the assumption that they were illusions. But he felt that if he himself half doubted his own story the rest of the world would disbelieve it completely. He decided to hold his tongue, and there the matter would have rested but for a very curious coincidence.

This is where I come into the story. I had known Dr. Ransom slightly for several years and corresponded with him on literary and philological subjects, though we very seldom met. It was, therefore, quite in the usual order of things that I should write him a letter some months ago, of which I will quote the relevant paragraph. It ran like this:

'I am now working at the Platonists of the twelfth century and incidentally discovering that they wrote damnably difficult Latin. In one of them, Bernardus Silvestris, there is a word I should particularly like your views on—the word *Oyarses*. It occurs in the description of a voyage through the heavens, and an *Oyarses* seems to be the "intelligence" or tutelary spirit of a heavenly sphere, i. e. in our language, of a planet. I asked C. J. about it and he says it ought to be *Ousiarches*. That, of course, would make sense, but I do not feel quite satisfied. Have you by any chance ever come across a word like *Oyarses,* or can you hazard any guess as to what language it may be?'

The immediate result of this letter was an invitation to spend a week-end with Dr. Ransom. He told me his whole story, and since then he and I have been almost continuously at work on the mystery. A good many facts, which I have no intention of publishing at present, have fallen into our hands; facts about planets in general and about Mars in particular, facts about mediæval Platonists, and (not least in importance) facts about the Professor to whom I am giving the fictitious name of Weston. A systematic report of these facts might, of course, be given to the civilized world: but that would almost certainly result in universal incredulity and in a libel action from 'Weston.' At the same time, we both feel that we cannot be silent. We are being daily confirmed in our belief that the *oyarses* of Mars was right when it said that the present 'celestial year' was to be a revolutionary one, that the long isolation of our own planet is nearing its end, and that great doings are on foot. We have found reason to believe that the mediæval Platonists were living in the same celestial year as ourselves— in fact, that it began in the twelfth century of our era—and that the occurrence of the name Oyarsa (Latinized as *oyarses*) in Bernardus Silvestris is not an accident. And we have also evidence—increasing almost daily—that 'Weston,' or the force or forces behind 'Weston,' will play a very important part in the events of the next few centuries, and, unless we prevent them, a very disastrous one. We do not mean that they are likely to invade Mars—our cry is not merely 'Hands off Malacandra.' The dangers to be feared are not planetary but cosmic, or at least solar, and they are not temporal but eternal. More than this it would be unwise to say.

It was Dr. Ransom who first saw that our only chance was to publish in the form of *fiction* what would certainly not be listened to as fact. He even thought—greatly overrating my literary powers—that this might have the incidental advantage of reaching a wider public, and that, certainly, it would reach a great many people sooner than 'Weston.' To my objection that if accepted as fiction it would for that very reason be regarded as false, he replied that there would be indications enough in the narrative for the few readers—the very few—who at *present* were prepared to go further into the matter.

'And they,' he said, 'will easily find out you, or me, and will easily identify Weston. Anyway,' he continued, 'what we need for the moment is not so much a body of belief as a body of people familiarized with certain ideas. If we could even effect in one per cent of our readers a change-over from the conception of Space to the conception of Heaven, we should have made a beginning.'

What neither of us foresaw was the rapid march of events which was to render the book out of date before it was published. These events have already made it rather a prologue to our story than the story itself. But we must let it go as it stands. For the later stages of the adventure—well, it was Aristotle, long before Kipling, who taught us the formula, 'That is another story.'

# Postscript

*(Being extracts from a letter written by the original of
'Dr. Ransom' to the author.)*

. . . I THINK you are right, and after the two or three correc-
tions (marked in red) the MS. will have to stand. I won't deny
that I am disappointed, but then any attempt to tell such a
story is bound to disappoint the man who has really been
there. I am not now referring to the ruthless way in which you
have cut down all the philological part, though, as it stands,
we are giving our readers a mere caricature of the Malacandrian
language. I mean something more difficult—something which
I couldn't possibly express. How can one 'get across' the Malacandrian *smells?* Nothing comes back to me more vividly in
my dreams . . . especially the early morning smell in those
purple woods, where the very mention of 'early morning' and
'woods' is misleading because it must set you thinking of earth
and moss and cobwebs and the smell of our planet, but I'm
thinking of something totally different. More 'aromatic' . . .
yes, but then it is not hot or luxurious or exotic as that word
suggests. Something aromatic, spicy, yet very cold, very thin,
tingling at the back of the nose—something that did to the
sense of smell what high, sharp violin notes do to the ear. And
mixed with that I always hear the sound of the singing—great
hollow hound-like music from enormous throats, deeper than
Chaliapin, a 'warm, dark noise.' I am homesick for my old
Malacandrian valley when I think of it; yet God knows when
I heard it there I was homesick enough for the Earth.

Of course you are right; if we are to treat it as a story you
*must* telescope the time I spent in the village during which
'nothing happened.' But I grudge it. Those quiet weeks, the
mere living among the *hrossa,* are to me the main thing that
happened. I *know* them, Lewis; that's what you can't get into
a mere story. For instance, because I always take a thermometer with me on a holiday (it has saved many a one from
being spoiled) I know that the normal temperature of a *hross*
is 103°. I know—though I can't remember learning it—that

155

they live about 80 Martian years, or 160 earth years; that they marry at about 20 (=40); that their droppings, like those of the horse, are not offensive to themselves, or to me, and are used for agriculture; that they don't shed tears, or blink; that they do get (as you would say) 'elevated' but not drunk on a gaudy night—of which they have many. But what can one do with these scraps of information? I merely analyse them out of a whole living memory that can never be put into words, and no one in this world will be able to build up from such scraps quite the right picture. For example, can I make even you understand how I know, beyond all question, why it is that the Malacandrians don't keep pets and, in general, don't feel about their 'lower animals' as we do about ours? Naturally it is the sort of thing they themselves could never have told me. One just sees why when one sees the three species together. Each of them is to the others *both* what a man is to us *and* what an animal is to us. They can talk to each other, they can cooperate, they have the same ethics; to that extent a *sorn* and a *hross* meet like two men. But then each finds the other different, funny, attractive as an animal is attractive. Some instinct starved in us, which we try to soothe by treating irrational creatures almost as if they were rational, is really satisfied in Malacandra. They don't need pets.

By the way, while we are on the subject of species, I am rather sorry that the exigencies of the story have been allowed to simplify the biology so much. Did I give you the impression that each of the three species was perfectly homogeneous? If so, I misled you. Take the *hrossa;* my friends were black *hrossa,* but there are also silver *hrossa,* and in some of the western *handramits* one finds the great crested *hross*—ten feet high, a dancer rather than a singer, and the noblest animal, after man, that I have ever seen. Only the males have the crest. I also saw a pure white *hross* at Meldilorn, but like a fool I never found out whether he represented a sub-species or was a mere freak like our terrestrial *albino.* There is at least one other kind of *sorn* besides the kind I saw—the *soroborn* or red *sorn* of the desert, who lives in the sandy north. He's a corker by all accounts.

I agree, it is a pity I never saw the *pfifltriggi* at home. I know nearly enough about them to 'fake' a visit to them as an episode in the story, but I don't think we ought to introduce any mere fiction. 'True in substance' sounds all very well on earth, but I can't imagine myself explaining it to Oyarsa, and I have a shrewd suspicion (see my last letter) that I have not heard the end of *him*. Anyway, why should our 'readers' (you seem to know the devil of a lot about them!), who are so determined to hear nothing about the language, be so anxious to know more of the *pfifltriggi*? But if you can work it in, there is, of course, no harm in explaining that they are oviparous and matriarchal, and short-lived compared with the other species. It is pretty plain that the great depressions which they inhabit are the old ocean-beds of Malacandra. *Hrossa*, who had visited them, described themselves as going down into deep forests over sand, 'the bone-stones (fossils) of ancient wave-borers about them.' No doubt these are the dark patches seen on the Martian disk from Earth. And that reminds me— the 'maps' of Mars which I have consulted since I got back are so inconsistent with one another that I have given up the attempt to identify my own *handramit*. If you want to try your hand, the desideratum is 'a roughly north-east and south-west "canal" cutting a north and south "canal" not more than twenty miles from the equator.' But astronomers differ very much as to what they can see.

Now as to your most annoying question: 'Did Augray, in describing the *eldila*, confuse the ideas of a subtler body and a superior being?' No. The confusion is entirely your own. He said two things: that the *eldila* had bodies different from those of planetary animals, and that they were superior in intelligence. Neither he nor anyone else in Malacandra ever confused the one statement with the other or deduced the one from the other. In fact, I have reasons for thinking that there are also irrational animals with the *eldil* type of body (you remember Chaucer's 'airish beasts'?).

I wonder are you wise to say nothing about the problem of *eldil* speech? I agree that it would spoil the narrative to raise the question during the trial-scene at Meldilorn, but surely many readers will have enough sense to ask how the *eldila*, who obviously don't breathe, can talk. It is true that we should have to admit we don't know, but oughtn't the readers to be told that? I suggested to J.—the only scientist here who is in my confidence—your theory that they might have instruments, or even organs, for manipulating the air around them and thus producing sounds indirectly, but he didn't seem to think much of it. He thought it probable that they directly manipulated the ears of those they were 'speaking' to. That sounds pretty difficult . . . of course one must remember that we have really no knowledge of the shape or size of an *eldil*, or even of its relations to space (*our* space) in general. In fact, one wants to keep on insisting that we really know next to nothing about them. Like you, I can't help trying to fix their relation to the things that appear in terrestrial tradition—gods, angels, fairies. But we haven't the data. When I attempted to give Oyarsa some idea of our own Christian angelology, he certainly seemed to regard our 'angels' as different in some way from himself. But whether he meant that they were a different species, or only that they were some special military caste (since our poor old earth turns out to be a kind of Ypres Salient in the universe), I don't know.

Why must you leave out my account of how the shutter jammed just before our landing on Malacandra? Without this, your description of our sufferings from excessive light on the return journey raises the very obvious question, 'Why didn't they close their shutters?' I don't believe your theory that 'readers never notice that sort of thing.' I'm sure I should.

There are two scenes that I wish you could have worked into the book; no matter—they are worked into me. One or other of them is always before me when I close my eyes.

In one of them I see the Malacandrian sky at morning; pale blue, so pale that now, when I have grown once more accustomed to terrestrial skies, I think of it as almost white. Against it the nearer tops of the giant weeds—the 'trees' as you call them—show black, but far away, across miles of that blinding blue water, the remoter woods are water-colour purple. The shadows all around me on the pale forest floor are like shadows on snow. There are figures walking before me; slender yet gigantic forms, black and sleek as animated tall hats; their huge round heads, poised on their sinuous stalk-like bodies, give them the appearance of black tulips. They go down, singing, to the edge of the lake. The music fills the wood with its vibration, though it is so soft that I can hardly hear it: it is like dim organ music. Some of them embark, but most remain. It is done slowly; this is no ordinary embarkation, but some ceremony. It is, in fact, a *hross* funeral. Those three with the grey muzzles whom they have helped into the boat are going to Meldilorn to die. For in that world, except for some few whom the *hnakra* gets, no one dies before his time. All live out the full span allotted to their kind, and a death with them is as predictable as a birth with us. The whole village has known that those three will die this year, this month; it was an easy guess that they would die even this week. And now they are off, to receive the last counsel of Oyarsa, to die, and to be by him 'unbodied.' The corpses, as corpses, will exist only for a few minutes: there are no coffins in Malacandra, no sextons, churchyards, or undertakers. The valley is solemn at their departure, but I see no signs of passionate grief. They do not doubt their immortality, and friends of the same generation are not torn apart. You leave the world, as you entered it, with the 'men of your own year.' Death is not preceded by dread nor followed by corruption.

The other scene is a nocturne. I see myself bathing with Hyoi in the warm lake. He laughs at my clumsy swimming; accustomed to a heavier world, I can hardly get enough of me under the water to make any headway. And then I see the night sky. The greater part of it is very like ours, though the depths are blacker and the stars brighter; but something that no terrestrial analogy will enable you fully to picture is happening in the west. Imagine the Milky Way magnified—the Milky Way seen through our largest telescope on the clearest night. And then imagine this, not painted across the zenith, but rising like a constellation behind the mountain-tops—a dazzling necklace of lights brilliant as planets, slowly heaving itself up till it fills a fifth of the sky and now leaves a belt of blackness between itself and the horizon. It is too bright to look at for long, but it is only a preparation. Something else is coming. There is a glow like moonrise on the *harandra*. *Ahihra!* cries Hyoi, and other baying voices answer him from the darkness all about us. And now the true king of night is set up, and now he is threading his way through that strange western galaxy and making its lights dim by comparison with his own. I turn my eyes away, for the little disk is far brighter than the Moon in her greatest splendour. The whole *handramit* is bathed in colourless light; I could count the stems of the forest on the far side of the lake; I see that my fingernails are broken and dirty. And now I guess what it is that I have seen —Jupiter rising beyond the Asteroids and forty million miles nearer than he has even been to earthly eyes. But the Malacandrians would say 'within the Asteroids,' for they have an odd habit, sometimes, of turning the solar system inside out. They call the Asteroids the 'dancers before the threshold of the Great Worlds.' The Great Worlds are the planets, as we should say, 'beyond' or 'outside' the Asteroids. Glundandra (Jupiter) is the greatest of these and has some importance in Malacandrian thought which I cannot fathom. He is 'the centre,' 'great Meldilorn,' 'throne' and 'feast.' They are, of course, well aware that he is uninhabitable, at least by animals of the planetary type; and they certainly have no pagan idea of giving a local habitation to Maleldil. But somebody or something of great importance is connected with Jupiter; as usual 'The *séroni* would know.' But they never told me. Perhaps the best comment is in the author whom I mentioned to you: 'For as it was well said of the great Africanus that he was never less alone than when alone, so, in our philosophy, no parts of this universal frame are less to be called solitarie than those which the vulgar esteem most solitarie, since the withdrawing of men and beasts signifieth but the greater frequency of more excellent creatures.'

More of this when you come. I am trying to read every old book on the subject that I can hear of. Now that 'Weston' has shut the door, the way to the planets lies through the past; if there is to be any more space-travelling, it will have to be time-travelling as well . . . !